"I've Seen You In The Morning, Claire,"

Nick rallied quickly. "Lots of times, if you'll recall."

"More than a decade ago," Claire hastened to add.

"Yeah, and you look even better now than you did then."

"Oh, right," Claire remarked. But she couldn't stop the warm fizzle of heat that wandered through her entire body at his words, at his look. Gee, waking up every morning to have a man like that give you a look like that… Well, it was certainly something a woman could get used to, Claire thought.

Of course, she shouldn't get used to it.

She couldn't get used to it.

She *wouldn't* get used to it.

Dear Reader,

Please join us in celebrating Silhouette's 20th anniversary in 2000! We promise to deliver—all year—passionate, powerful, provocative love stories from your favorite Desire authors!

This January, look for bestselling author Leanne Banks's first MAN OF THE MONTH with *Her Forever Man.* Watch sparks fly when irresistibly rugged ranch owner Brock Logan comes face-to-face with his new partner, the fiery Felicity Chambeau, in the first book of Leanne's brand-new miniseries LONE STAR FAMILIES: THE LOGANS.

Desire is pleased to continue the Silhouette cross-line continuity ROYALLY WED with *The Pregnant Princess* by favorite author Anne Marie Winston. After a night of torrid passion with a stranger, a beautiful princess ends up pregnant…and seeks out the father of her child.

Elizabeth Bevarly returns to Desire with her immensely popular miniseries FROM HERE TO MATERNITY with *Dr. Mommy,* about a couple reunited by a baby left on a doorstep. *Hard Lovin' Man,* another of Peggy Moreland's TEXAS BRIDES, captures the intensity of falling in love when a cowgirl gives her heart to a sweet-talkin', hard-lovin' hunk. Cathleen Galitz delivers a compelling marriage-of-convenience tale in *The Cowboy Takes a Bride,* in the series THE BRIDAL BID. And Sheri WhiteFeather offers another provocative Native American hero in *Skyler Hawk: Lone Brave.*

Help us celebrate 20 years of great romantic fiction from Silhouette by indulging yourself with all six delectably sensual Desire titles each and every month during this special year!

Enjoy!

Joan Marlow Golan
Senior Editor, Silhouette Desire

Please address questions and book requests to:
Silhouette Reader Service
U.S.: 3010 Walden Ave., P.O. Box 1325, Buffalo, NY 14269
Canadian: P.O. Box 609, Fort Erie, Ont. L2A 5X3

Dr. Mommy

ELIZABETH BEVARLY

Silhouette® Desire®

Published by Silhouette Books

America's Publisher of Contemporary Romance

For David,
Slayer of icky bugs,
Finder of lost computer files,
Stay-at-home dad,
Perfect husband.

Thanks, Sweetie.

 SILHOUETTE BOOKS

ISBN 0-373-76269-0

DR. MOMMY

Visit us at www.romance.net

Printed in U.S.A.

Books by Elizabeth Bevarly

Silhouette Desire

An Unsuitable Man for the Job #724
Jake's Christmas #753
A Lawless Man #856
*A Dad Like Daniel #908
*The Perfect Father #920
*Dr. Daddy #933
†Father of the Brat #993
†Father of the Brood #1005
†Father on the Brink #1016
‡Roxy and the Rich Man #1053
‡Lucy and the Loner #1063
‡Georgia Meets Her Groom #1083
**Bride of the Bad Boy #1124
**Beauty and the Brain #1130
**The Virgin and the Vagabond #1136
The Sheriff and the Impostor Bride #1184
††Society Bride #1196
That Boss of Mine #1231
*A Doctor in Her Stocking #1252
*Dr. Mommy #1269

Silhouette Special Edition

Destinations South #557
Close Range #590
Donovan's Chance #639
Moriah's Mutiny #676
Up Close #737
Hired Hand #803
Return Engagement #844

*From Here to Maternity
†From Here to Paternity
‡The Family McCormick
**Blame It on Bob
††Fortune's Children:
    The Brides

ELIZABETH BEVARLY

is an honors graduate of the University of Louisville and achieved her dream of writing full-time before she even turned thirty! At heart, she is also an avid voyager who once helped navigate a friend's thirty-five-foot sailboat across the Bermuda Triangle. Her dream is to one day have her own sailboat, a beautifully renovated older-model forty-two-footer, and to enjoy the freedom and tranquillity seafaring can bring. Elizabeth likes to think she has a lot in common with the characters she creates, people who know love and life go hand in hand. And she's getting some firsthand experience with mother-hood, as well—she and her husband have a five-year-old son, Eli.

IT'S OUR 20th ANNIVERSARY!
We'll be celebrating all year,
starting with these fabulous titles,
on sale in January 2000.

One

Dick Clark had just announced that there was less than five minutes left to this *New Year's Rockin' Eve* when Dr. Claire Wainwright heard the chime of her front doorbell erupt downstairs. Ignoring the interruption—doubtless it was just some New Year's reveler playing a joke, because heaven knew she wasn't expecting anyone—she noted that Dick, as always, looked suave and cheerful and eternally young. And she tried not to dwell on the fact that she herself felt…well, not. Not suave. Not cheerful. Not eternally young.

Au contraire, Claire.

When the doorbell chimed again, she exhaled an errant sigh and waited to see if maybe, possibly, perchance, hopefully, she had only imagined the doleful, lonely sounds of that single, solitary *dingdong*. Because—speaking of doleful and lonely—she had just settled into bed with a flute of flat-going champagne, had just opened the latest issue of

JAMA to an article about C-sections and had just gotten as comfortable as she was likely to be in this lifetime. And—speaking of single and solitary—she was home alone. On New Year's Eve. Again.

Of course—speaking of dingdong—she could have accepted that one offer of a New Year's Eve date that she *had* received, but *noooo*…

Claire still wasn't sure what had possessed her to turn down Evan Duran's invitation to spend the evening with him at his cottage in Cape May. It would have been a lovely, lovely event, she told herself now. Snowy moonlight on the ocean, a fire crackling merrily in the hearth, lobster and pâté and champagne every bit as good as what she'd bought for her own solitary celebration.

Of course, the evening would have inevitably stretched into the night, she thought further. And, of course, Evan would have been there, too. Which, now that she thought about it, was doubtless why she had declined his offer.

Nevertheless, he was a handsome, intelligent, decent guy, she reminded herself, a man who had a *lot* of ambition and drive. He was exactly the kind of man who should interest her, the kind of man with whom she should spend the rest of her life. She didn't know why she found him so unappealing. There was just nothing there—no spark, no heat, no magic.

The doorbell chimed a third time from way downstairs, and Claire told herself it would be pointless to try to ignore it any longer. Still, she was more than a little puzzled by who might be summoning her at such an hour on such a night. Shoving back the plush, pale blue comforter, she ran one hand through her straight, black, shoulder-length hair, smoothed the other over her amethyst-colored silk pajamas, then tucked her feet into the slippers by her bed. She wasn't working, obviously, but that didn't mean she was free to do as she pleased with her time off. An OB-GYN's work was never done, Claire knew, and babies didn't exactly come on schedule.

But she wasn't accustomed to having her patients show up at her house in Haddonfield, either. If an expectant mom found herself on the brink of delivery, she usually went to Seton General Hospital in neighboring Cherry Hill. If Claire wasn't on call—and tonight, she wasn't—then one of the other four doctors with whom she was in practice delivered the baby. All of her patients knew that. And it was a system that worked well.

Except when people rang her doorbell at midnight on New Year's Eve.

Unable to fully shake her wariness, she thrust her arms through the sleeves of the tailored silk robe that matched her tailored silk pajamas, then made her way down the long hallway and curving staircase of the roomy, exuberant Tudor she had bought nearly a year ago. Still not quite over the fear of the dark she'd had when she was a child, Claire kept night-lights placed strategically throughout the house, so she found her way now with little trouble. But the fine antique furnishings that were so posh and elegant in daylight seemed looming and a bit overwhelming in the dark. With a nervous gesture, she cinched the belt of her robe a bit tighter.

The doorbell chimed again as her foot hit the thick Persian rug at the bottom of the stairs, in the expansive foyer. Through the stained-glass panes of the front door across from her, Claire made out the silhouette of someone who appeared to be about the same stature and height as she— five-foot-five. In low heels. On a good day.

In the living room to the left of the front door, beyond the beveled bay windows overlooking her front lawn, she noted that the snow that had begun earlier as a soft, powdery cascade had ripened into a full-blown storm. Fat wet flakes blew in fierce sideways slants, buffeting the house with a rattling wind that virtually shook the place. Claire shuddered, even though it was plenty warm inside, and she wondered again what would bring someone to her front door on such a night.

She turned in that direction again, then hesitated when she realized the silhouette had disappeared. Funny, that. Or perhaps not. Maybe whoever had rung the bell had been a bit tipsy, and had finally discovered they had the wrong house. Maybe they had left in embarrassment before being discovered.

Or maybe they hadn't.

Just to be certain, Claire continued on to the front door and peeked through one of the uncolored panes on the side. But through the flawed, crackled glass, she saw only a swirl of white snow dancing haphazardly in the pale yellow glow of her porch light. She was about to turn away when her gaze lit on a figure at the foot of her driveway.

There was indeed someone out there, someone whose attention was focused fully on Claire as she peeked outside. Someone who, she noted further, had left tracks in the nearly six inches of snow that had accumulated on the walk between the driveway and her front door since she'd paid her neighbor's teenager to shovel it earlier that afternoon.

A ripple of apprehension shimmied up Claire's spine at the sight of the other person, and she immediately swept her hand over the panel of switches on the wall to her right. Instantly the front yard was flooded with light—from the lamp by the driveway, the lights over the garage and a row of lanterns lining the landscaped walk and drive.

In that brief moment, Claire saw that the person outside appeared to be a young woman wearing a black jacket and black beret, with long blond hair cascading over her shoulders. But as soon as the exterior lights flashed on, the young woman turned and fled across the street, stumbling only once in the heavy snow. There she slowed, evidently feeling safer under cover of darkness. But she turned to walk slowly backward and continued to gaze at Claire's house, as if she were hesitant to leave.

Very odd, Claire thought. And not a little troubling.

She was trying to decide whether or not the episode warranted calling the police—oh, surely not—when she realized there was something else outside, too. A large, oval, handled basket sat atop the snow at the foot of the creekstone steps leading to the front door, its contents already dusted liberally with snow. Contents that appeared to be…laundry?

Why would someone leave a basket of laundry on her doorstep on New Year's Eve? Claire wondered. That made no sense at all. She had lived in South Jersey since her freshman year of high school, and although there were certainly some interesting traditions indigenous to this part of the country, leaving laundry on someone's doorstep to celebrate the new year wasn't one of them.

Come to think of it, that wasn't a tradition in any of the dozens of cultures Claire had called home at one time or another, growing up as she had, the daughter of doctors who were serving as Peace Corps volunteers.

She was still wracking her brain for some explanation when, to her surprise and horror, the bundle of fabric inside the basket moved, and a tiny, mittened fist poked itself free of the blanket surrounding it. Claire realized then that the basket contained, not laundry, but a baby.

Oh, no. No, no, no, no, no…

With two swift gestures, she freed the chain and dead bolt on the front door, then tugged it open wide and stepped outside, frantically searching the opposite side of the street for the young woman who had stood on her driveway only a moment before. Sure enough, the black-clad figure was there, halfway down the block now, staring back at the house. But when she saw Claire come outside, saw her descend the stairs toward the basket, the woman turned and fled with all her might, as if the hounds of hell were following her.

Oh, no. No, no, no, no, no…

This couldn't be happening, Claire thought. Surely she was dreaming. Surely this was some kind of joke. Some really sick, twisted kind of joke, but a joke nonetheless. Surely her colleagues at the hospital—the ones who knew how she felt about children—would jump out of the shrubbery anytime now, and they'd all have a good, if sick and twisted, laugh at her expense.

Surely.

Then Claire heard a small, soft sound, like the coo of a dove, and gazed down at the basket again. This time, when the fabric moved, she saw a pair of pale blue eyes peeking out from beneath the cuff of a pink knit cap. For a few seconds, she only gazed at those eyes and shook her head in disbelief. Then a particularly fat, particularly wet snowflake smacked her in the eye. She realized then that her toes were freezing in their scant satin slippers, and that her warm silk pajamas had turned icy as they clung to her skin.

And she realized that this wasn't a joke, sick and twisted or otherwise. So she bent down and looped her arm through the two handles on the basket and gingerly lifted it. Then, stepping carefully over the piles of snow on her front steps, she carried the baby back into the house, closing and bolting the door behind her.

Don't panic, she instructed herself as, heart racing, limbs trembling, she leaned back against the front door and wondered what to do—besides panic.

Think, Claire. Think. Breathe, relax and think.

But the muddled thoughts tumbling through her brain scattered hastily when the baby in the basket began to make noise again. Nothing alarming, just some quiet little murmurs of…of…of baby noise, sounds that gave her the impression that the child was, for the moment, content. That, however, could change anytime, she told herself. So she'd better figure out what on earth she was going to do.

Police, she thought. Yeah, that's it. She should call the police. They'd know how to treat a situation like this. Certainly better than she would. Although she was an OB-GYN, she wasn't too familiar with babies. Not once they'd entered the world, anyway. That, of course, was where the pediatricians stepped in. And thank God for that. Claire was fascinated by the generation and growth of life inside the womb. But once those little nippers came out, well… She was grateful to be able to wash her hands of them. Literally.

It wasn't that she didn't like children. They were just a completely alien life force, as far as she was concerned. She'd been an only child of two only children, so she hadn't been exposed to any babies growing up. And because she and her parents had moved around a lot, to cultures that changed as quickly as their residences did, Claire had never really learned to relate to other children for any length of time. She'd been shy and anxious when she'd come to new communities, and as a result, she'd remained fairly solitary. She'd just never much abided children. Not even when she was a child herself.

And now here she was, face-to-face with a baby—a *baby!*—and she had no idea what to do. Okay, of course, she knew the basics, that they needed to be fed and diapered and kept warm. Which, now that she thought about it, might be a good reason to panic, because she had neither baby food nor diapers in her house. Then again, the basket on her arm was a bit larger and heavier than seemed necessary for one baby. Could be that whomever had abandoned the little tyke had at least properly provided for it.

For the time being, anyway, she added to herself, swallowing the panic that began to rise yet again.

She forced herself to move to the overstuffed couch on the other side of the living room, then switched on the standing Tiffany lamp beside it and settled the basket carefully down between two big tapestry pillows. Nudging aside the bulk of blankets in which the baby had been swaddled—okay, so the keeping warm part would be no problem—Claire found, in addition to the pudgy infant, about three dozen diapers, a can of powdered formula, four small bottles, an assortment of baby food in jars and five changes of clothes, all pink.

Congratulations, Claire. It's a girl.

"Oh, boy," she muttered to no one in particular.

Until now she had been trying to avoid actually looking at the baby, but when the infant began to chatter incoherently again, Claire had no choice but to turn her attention to the little cherub. She had no idea how old the tiny thing was, but the baby was smiling and attentive and making a lot of noise, so she must be several months old, anyway. As Claire watched, the infant's mouth formed a near-perfect O, and she released a long, lusty coo. Then she laughed, as if she'd just made a wonderful joke, and for a moment—just a moment—Claire felt sort of, kind of… warm inside, and she smiled back.

Then she remembered she had no idea how to care for this child and that ripple of panic began to surge up inside her again.

"Police," she whispered aloud, as if needing an audible reminder. Surely the police could send someone over right away, someone who knew what to do with abandoned babies, someone who could see to this particular baby's needs better than Claire could herself. Because although there were a lot of things in her life about which she felt uncertain, of one thing she was absolutely sure. She was in no way cut out to be a mother. Nuh-uh. No way. No how.

As if she needed to be reassured of that fact—which, of course, she didn't—when she reached in to lift the baby out of the basket, it immediately began to howl. Loudly. Lustily. Lengthily.

Okay, Claire. You can panic now.

Oh, boy, she thought. It was going to be a long night.

Nick Campisano was just leaving his favorite liquor store with a six-pack of his favorite brew when his pager went off.

Great, he thought. He should have realized there was no way he'd be allowed to enjoy what was left of New Year's Eve. Hey, he hadn't been allowed to enjoy Christmas Eve, had he? Or Christmas, either. Or Thanksgiving, for that matter. Or even Halloween, dammit. In fact, he couldn't remember the last time he'd been allowed to have an entire holiday off at all. So why should tonight be any different?

Because he needed a break, dammit—that was why. He needed a little time to step back and reevaluate, and try to remember why he'd become a cop in the first place. Something about wanting to make a difference, he recalled from some vague, dark, corner of his mind. Something about wanting to be a role model for kids who didn't have any in their lives. Something about wanting to help people— help kids—get themselves straight and stay that way.

Yeah, right, he thought now. As a narcotics detective, all he seemed to succeed in doing lately was watch the problem get worse. Too many kids—good kids, at that—were taking drugs, selling drugs, dying from drugs. Oh, yeah. Nick had made a really big difference for them.

And tonight—like every other night—he needed some time to unwind and relax, some time to think about life. Some time to help him remember what living *his* life was all about. Yeah, life, he echoed derisively to himself. He was gonna have to see about getting himself one of those real soon. All work and no play was making Nick a very cranky boy.

He sighed with resignation when he noted the number on his pager, then made his way slowly back to his big— and very dated—Jeep Wagoneer, where he'd left his cell phone for the few minutes he'd be inside Cavanaugh's Liquors. Sure enough, the word *Called* appeared in the readout. Clearing it, Nick punched in the number he'd been instructed to return—the number of his workplace—and after hearing a feminine voice greet him blandly at the other end of the line, he snarled, "Campisano. Whaddaya want?"

"Woooo, those are just the words a woman wants to hear in the middle of the night from a big, strong man like you," the sultry voice at the other end of the line said, punctuating the observation with a wry chuckle.

"Sorry, Lieutenant," Nick said—even if it was without a trace of apology. Suzanne Skolnik was, after all, his boss, but she wasn't so far removed that he couldn't voice his irritation at being summoned during his off-hours. "Whaddaya want?"

"Where are you?" she asked without preamble.

"Halfway home. Soon I'll be all the way home," he added pointedly. "Why?"

But instead of answering his question, she said, "Define 'halfway home.'"

Nick growled under his breath. This didn't sound good.

"Cavanaugh's Liquors on Route 30," he told her. Then he asked again, "Why?"

"So you're skirting the wilds of Haddonfield, right?"

Nick growled again. "Yeah. Why?"

"And you got four-wheel drive in that big bucket of yours, right?"

"Yeah. *Why?*"

But he still didn't get a response to the one question he really wanted answered. Not a response that he liked anyway. Because his superior asked another question of her own. "You know a lot about kids, don't you, Nick?"

As questions went, it wasn't that unusual a one for a man in his line of work to hear. "I know enough," he said. "Why?"

"Don't you got, like, a lot of nieces and nephews?"

"Eighteen, last count," he replied. *"Why?"*

"That's right," Lieutenant Skolnik said thoughtfully. "Your sister Angie just dropped two last month, didn't she?"

Nick was fast losing patience with this interrogation. Not just because he seldom indulged in chitchat with his boss, but because he was cold, and he was tired, and the snow was coming down harder and at least two of the six bottles of Sam Adams in the seat next to him were calling his name.

"Uh, no offense, Lieutenant," he said slowly, "but, um…I'd appreciate it if you could tell me just where the hell this line of questioning is going."

"I need you to answer a call for me in Haddonfield," she said finally.

"Oh, *come on*," he pleaded, even though he knew it was pointless to try. "I just pulled a double shift, and I haven't had a day off in two weeks. I'm supposed to have three days off solid. You promised, and I earned it."

"I know, Nick, and I'm really sorry," she said, her voice conveying her genuine apology. "But you're the only one who can take care of this."

He grumbled something unintelligible under his breath. Then aloud he said, "Define 'this.'"

"We got a report of an abandoned baby in Haddonfield," she told him. "And we got nobody in the area who can respond right now. Since you just left here twenty minutes ago, and since I know your proclivities regarding Cavanaugh's," she added parenthetically, "I figured I could catch you in the area."

Before he could object further, she gave him the exact address, and Nick whistled low. "That's a pretty primo rent district. Who'd be abandoning a baby there?"

Wryly his lieutenant replied, "Gee, just a shot in the dark here, but...maybe somebody who can't take care of it and wants it to have a better life?"

Nick rolled his eyes. "Even if it means breaking the law to get it?"

"Yeah, well, believe it or not, Nick, there are some people out there who hold the laws of our great state in contempt. I know that comes as a shock to a guy like you, but..."

"Yeah, yeah, yeah," he muttered. "So, why do I get the assignment? I kinda had other plans."

Not that those plans consisted of anything major, he conceded to himself. Just a little sleeping and eating and watching what was left of *Saturday Night Dead* with Stellaaaa— not necessarily in that order. But there was no reason his lieutenant had to know that.

"You get the job," she told him, "because, like I said, between the New Year's revelers and the snow, we can't get anybody else out there tonight. And nobody at Social Services is answering the phone right now. Dispatch says the woman who made the report sounds pretty frantic. Says she can't take care of the baby. So somebody's gotta go get that kid. You're a couple miles away. You got four-wheel drive. You can swing by there and take care of it and, even with the paperwork, be home by morning. Then, I promise you, you can have *four* days. Solid.''

Being home by morning, Nick thought, was highly debatable. Not only was morning barely seven hours away, but the way the snow was coming down, it wouldn't be long before even four-wheel drive would be totally ineffective. Still, it would be nice to get an extra day off out of this. And he *was* only a couple of miles away. And he *did* kind of have a soft spot for kids.

Dammit.

''All right, all right,'' he relented, however reluctantly. ''I'll take care of it as fast as I can. But those four days you promised? I better get every last one of 'em. Without being bothered once.''

''You got my word, Nick,'' Lieutenant Skolnick promised. ''Scout's honor.''

He told himself not to dwell on the fact that Suzanne Skolnik seemed in no way the Scout type, scribbled down the particulars of the reported abandonment, then ground the Wagoneer to life. Was it his imagination, or had the already fierce snowfall doubled in severity in the few minutes he'd spent on the phone? He shook the thought off. No problem. His Jeep was more than reliable, and he had little trouble maneuvering it over the snow and slush. In no time at all—well, not much time at all—Nick rolled to a halt in the driveway of the house to which he'd been directed.

Nice piece of real estate, he thought. Must have set the owners back a pretty penny, but then, people who lived in neighborhoods like this one usually didn't have to worry too much about paying the bills. The place was lit up outside like a Christmas tree, and Nick could tell that when it wasn't snowing like a big dog, it was probably a real showplace, carefully landscaped and tended. A big two-story monstrosity, it had the look of English aristocracy about it, with bay windows leaded in a diamond pattern, and stained glass all around the front door. It was the kind of place that was perfectly suited for big garden parties and intimate tea socials.

In other words, it was about as far removed from Nick's own personal reality as it could possibly be.

As a South Jersey boy, born and bred, he was blue-collar in the extreme. And damned proud of it, too. His father had been a cop, just like his father's father had been, and his father's father's father before that. All the Campisanos were either in law enforcement or fire fighting, and all the Gianellis, on his mom's side, worked in the Gianelli bakery. That's where Nick's mom had invariably been while he was growing up—when she wasn't seeing to the needs of her six kids.

Nick chuckled in spite of himself as he gazed at the big house before him. His family sure could have used that much square footage when he was growing up, but chances were the occupants of this house probably didn't have any kids at all. At most, they probably only claimed one or two. He'd shared a small bedroom with his two brothers the whole time he was growing up, and his three sisters had made do with another. The little brick bungalow in Gloucester City had only had one bathroom for the longest time, until his father and his uncle Leo had installed another one in the basement when the Campisano children started turning into Campisano teenagers.

What a luxury that had been, he recalled now with a

fond smile. Two bathrooms. No waiting. Not beyond twenty or thirty minutes, anyway.

Still, Nick wouldn't change a thing about his upbringing. Even though there had never been a dime to spare, and even though he and his brothers and sisters had all gone to work in one capacity or another when they turned sixteen, he'd never felt as though he lacked anything in life. The Campisanos were a close-knit bunch to this day, and it was no doubt because they'd learned to share and compromise at an early age.

Nick wouldn't have it any other way. There was nothing in the world, he knew, that was more important than family. Nothing.

He glanced down at the sheet of paper where he'd scrawled the information Lieutenant Skolnik had given him about the abandoned baby. The dispatcher had done her best to record the particulars accurately, but the woman calling in had obviously been more than a little upset, and the baby had evidently been squalling like a demon seed right next to the phone. Dr. Carrie Wayne was what the woman's name was. Nick just hoped this was the right house. Focusing on the big Tudor again, he decided that whatever kind of doctor she was, she must be damned good at it.

He shoved open the driver's side door, pushing hard against an especially brutal gust of wind, then he heaved himself out into the storm. The snow easily covered his heavy hiking boots—it must be almost a foot deep by now. He tugged up the zipper on his navy blue, down-filled parka, stuffed his hands into his heavy leather gloves and slung his hood up over his head. No sense courting pneumonia on top of too much work, he thought. Hey, he intended to enjoy those four days off he had coming.

By the time he trudged his way to the front door, he was

huffing and puffing with the effort it had taken to cover the short distance, thanks to the wind and snow. And he was thinking that he'd better get this over with quick if he had any hope of finishing by morning. He rapped his fist hard against the wooden part of the front door, then thought better of that and jabbed the doorbell twice. Then he took a step backward to wait. The howling of a baby greeted him from the other side—yep, it was the right house, all right—and then someone pulled the door inward. Nick opened his mouth to say something in greeting.

Opened it to say something in greeting, but not one single word came out.

Because once he saw who stood on the other side of that door, he couldn't speak at all. He couldn't breathe. He couldn't think. All he could do was stare at the black-haired, blue-eyed woman standing there, and remember how soft and fragrant was every single curve and valley that lay beneath those shiny purple pajamas she had on.

Not Dr. Carrie Wayne, he thought inanely. Dr. Claire Wainwright. As if he needed anything else to make this night more pointless and irritating than it already promised to be.

Two

The baby had been crying off and on ever since Claire had picked her up, but she'd gone absolutely ballistic at the sound of the doorbell. Yet even with a baby screeching in her ear, the moment Claire opened the door and saw Nick Campisano standing on the other side, she heard nothing but the roar of her blood rushing through her body.

Nick. God. Of all the people who could have shown up in response to her call, why did it have to be him?

Oh, sure, she knew he was a cop, and that he worked and lived within twenty minutes or so of her house. But never in her wildest dreams had it occurred to her that when she called the police to report an abandoned baby, Nick would be the one who'd show up to respond.

Why would they send a narcotics detective? she wondered. And if they did send a narcotics detective, then why did it have to be the one who'd taken her virginity more than fifteen years ago?

Oh, come on, Claire, she immediately chastised herself. *He didn't exactly take your virginity, did he? You pretty much wrapped it up with a big bow and gave it to him.*

She shoved the reminder away before it could become a memory, and forced herself to step backward into the house. Evidently needing no further invitation than that, Nick strode easily into the foyer, and she hastily closed the door behind him. She watched in silence—well, *she* was silent, anyway, even if the baby *was* still howling—as he shoved the hood back from his head and tugged off his gloves, his gaze never wavering from hers as he completed the actions. And she noted, too, that in the three years that had passed since she'd last seen him, Nick's dark hair had begun to go a bit gray.

That was the only sign of change on him, though. And even at that, there were merely a few brave threads of silver that had dared to appear in his coal-black hair. The rest of him looked pretty much the same as it had the last time she'd seen him—appealingly rugged, startlingly handsome, overwhelmingly self-assured. And big. Really, really big. How could she have forgotten the fact that he towered over her so? Even when she'd last seen him, when she was wearing high heels, his size had intimidated her.

Though it was funny, now that she thought about it— he'd never intimidated her when they'd been together. It had only been since they'd split up after college that Nick had seemed to become so…awesome.

Again she remembered their last encounter—what an awkward situation that had been. They'd bumped into each other at a wedding, of all places. And it had just been too painful a reminder of the way she'd turned down his proposal of marriage all those years ago.

He seemed to be thinking about those times, too, she noted, because his dark eyes were wary, his posture stiff and his mouth—that incredibly sexy, wholly masculine mouth—was turned down in a frown. Which was just as well, really. Because she recalled all too well just how positively breathtaking Nick Campisano could be when he smiled. Nick's smile...

She couldn't quite bite back a sigh at the memories that washed over her in a warm, wonderful wave. Nick's smile had always made everything in the world seem all right. It had also always brought her to her knees.

"Claire," he said carefully by way of a greeting, his voice reflecting no emotion whatsoever.

In spite of that, Claire nearly melted as quickly as the snow that was pooling around his big hiking boots. Oh, wow, she thought. Just the sound of her name uttered in his soft, velvety voice made the hairs at the back of her neck leap to life. Anything else he said, she could tell already, would rouse the rest of her body parts just as thoroughly, just as quickly.

"Nick," she managed to reply, albeit cautiously. But she was inordinately proud of herself for being able to voice even that one word without revealing the tumult of conflicting emotions that were warring inside her, just below the surface.

However, neither of them seemed to know what to say beyond those two single-syllable acknowledgments.

The baby, however, seemed to have a very good idea what to add. Although she had temporarily ceased her wailing when Nick had entered the foyer, the infant burst into tears again at the awkward, tension-filled silence that ensued. The reaction was completely appropriate, as far as Claire was concerned. She was beginning to feel like crying herself.

Automatically—though none too easily—she began to bounce the baby in her arms, but the gesture did nothing to soothe the poor thing's anxiety. On the contrary, the infant seemed to become even more agitated with Claire's attempt to comfort, and her wailing elevated to a full-blown screeching.

"Not like that," Nick said, unzipping his coat. Then he reached for the baby as if it were the most natural thing in the world for him to do.

Eagerly Claire released the infant to his care, and he settled it easily against the soft cotton sweater covering his chest. He splayed one big hand open over the baby's back—nearly covering it—then rubbed his palm in a leisurely circle, rocking his entire body back and forth with a slow, gentle rhythm. Almost immediately, the baby's crying eased up, then gradually diminished until she hiccuped with a soft sigh and stopped entirely.

"Shhh," Nick said quietly, never altering his motions. "It's okay, sweetheart. Nobody here is going to hurt you. You're just fine. Shhh…"

Even though she knew the reassurance was meant for the baby, somehow it went a long way toward making Claire feel better, too. "Thanks," she said. But whether her gratitude was for his calming the child's fears or her own, she couldn't rightly say.

Although Nick continued to croon soothing, comforting words to the baby, his gaze never wavered from hers, and a million accusations seemed to burn in the dark espresso depths of his eyes. She wished she could think of something to say that might make the situation a little more bearable. But for the life of her she couldn't even think of some meaningless platitude to utter.

For another long moment, the two of them only continued to stare at each other without speaking. Nick mumbled softly to the baby, and Claire stood uncomfortably with her arms crossed over her midsection, watching them. Watching the way his big body formed a protective shelter for the tiny life he held so carefully in his embrace. Watching the way his entire face seemed to soften and grow warm with the action of cuddling an infant. Watching how effortlessly, how naturally, he performed the action.

Eventually the sight of Nick and the baby grew too difficult for Claire to witness, so she turned around and left the foyer behind, making her way into the living room instead.

And she tried very hard not to think about the fact that, if things had turned out differently, she might very well be married to Nick right now. And the baby he cradled in his arms might very well be theirs.

Stop it, Claire, she admonished herself immediately. Things *hadn't* turned out differently. They *hadn't* gotten married, and that *wasn't* their baby in Nick's arms. She'd made her choices a long time ago, and now she had to live with them. Just because things hadn't exactly worked out the way she had thought they would, well... That was no reason to dwell on regrets and what-ifs.

Even if she and Nick *had* married back then, there was no guarantee they'd still be married today. Claire knew she wouldn't have been happy with the kind of life he had envisioned for them. And her unhappiness would have doubtless flowed over onto him. It was very likely that, by now, they both would have been miserable. They might not even be together anymore.

Thankfully her thoughts were interrupted when Nick followed her into the living room with the now-silent baby. When he strode past her, she saw that the infant had fallen asleep. Very carefully he bent to return the baby to its basket, then moved it to the floor in front of the couch. For a moment, he only watched the infant sleep, her little mouth working over a bottle that only existed in her dreams. Claire smiled warmly at the sight. Then Nick stood up and turned to face her, and her smile immediately vanished.

Without speaking, he tilted his head toward the other side of the room, where they could talk without fear of waking the baby. Claire preceded him in that direction, stopping by the fireplace, where, surprisingly, a few warm embers still glowed from the fire she had enjoyed earlier that evening.

He hadn't removed his big parka, but unzipping it had revealed beneath it a baggy, tobacco-colored sweater and well-worn jeans. Without even looking to see what he was doing, he withdrew a small notebook and ballpoint pen from the inside pocket, all the while gazing at her with bland expectation. The accusation that had darkened his eyes earlier was gone now, and his posture was no longer hostile. In many ways, it seemed to Claire that he had turned into a total stranger.

"So you want to tell me how all this came about?" he asked as he clicked the pen, the very picture of efficiency. Somehow, though, when he voiced the question, he seemed to be talking about a whole lot more than the baby who had just shown up on her doorstep.

Well, gosh, Nick, it's like this, Claire thought. *You wanted something totally different from what I wanted, and you never once stopped to ask me about* my *dreams and* my *desires. You could only think about your own, and you assumed I'd just go merrily along. That's how all this came about.*

She pushed the thought away before the words could spill out of her mouth and into the open, ensuring what would undoubtedly become an ugly scene. Instead, she scrunched up her shoulders restlessly and let them fall, sighed fitfully, then ran an unsteady hand through her hair.

"I was in bed when I heard the doorbell ring just before midnight," she began.

"Alone?" he demanded.

She couldn't quite help the incredulous little sound that escaped her. "Do you see anybody else here?" she countered.

"No," he conceded. "But that doesn't necessarily mean you're here alone."

"I'm alone," she muttered. Then, just because she felt spiteful, she added, "Tonight I am, anyway."

The verbal dart must have struck its target perfectly, because Nick's frown returned, and his eyes darkened angrily again. "Fine," he bit off. "You were alone in bed and heard the doorbell just before midnight. You sure about the time?"

She nodded. "Dick Clark had just updated me to the situation in Times Square," she said.

"Then what happened?"

"I ignored it at first," she continued. "I thought it was probably some New Year's Eve prank. But it happened a couple more times, so I finally got up to answer it."

"You make it a habit to answer your door in the middle of the night when you're here all alone?" he asked, not bothering to disguise the fact that he considered such behavior to be, well, pretty stupid.

"Hey, I don't usually *have* to answer the door in the middle of the night," she told him. She decided to let him sort out for himself whether that was because she didn't normally have visitors at that time of night, or because there was usually someone else here with her—someone of the masculine persuasion—who answered the door that time of night for her.

Before he could object further, she added, "I thought it might be a patient. And I didn't just run down and pull the door open wide in welcome. I checked through the window first. That was when I saw the woman standing at the foot of my driveway."

Nick narrowed his eyes at her. "You actually saw a woman leave the baby?"

Claire shook her head. "I didn't see her literally put the basket down on my doorstep, but I think it's a safe bet she's the one who left the baby here, yes."

"Did you get a good look at her?"

"Not really. It was dark, and it was snowing pretty hard, and the part of the window I was looking through isn't completely clear. But the brief glimpse I got of her gave me the impression that she was young. All I can tell you for certain is that she was white, had long blond hair, and was wearing a black jacket and beret. Those are about the only things I'm sure of."

Nick nodded slowly. "Did you speak to her at all?"

Again Claire shook her head. "As soon as I saw her out there, I switched on all the outdoor lights, but she took off running before I could see her clearly or say anything. For what it's worth, she did seem hesitant to go. Even after I came outside, she didn't bolt right away. Just slowed down on the other side of the street and watched me. It was only after she knew I saw the basket that she took off running. I think she wanted to make sure the baby was taken inside before she left."

Nick eyed her thoughtfully as he processed the information. "You sound like you're defending her actions."

Claire opened her mouth to protest, then closed it, putting some thought into her response before giving it. "Maybe I am, in a way," she relented. "Whoever the young woman was, she really did seem reluctant to leave. I don't think she would have abandoned the baby unless she was sure someone would be home to take it inside."

"It still doesn't excuse what she did."

"No, it doesn't," Claire agreed.

He paused a telling moment before adding sarcastically, "But I can see why you'd think her behavior was acceptable."

Okay, now that made Claire mad. "I never said her behavior was acceptable," she countered. "Don't put words in my mouth, Nick." She refrained from adding *again*.

"Yeah, but you're no fan of children, are you?" he charged.

"Hey, I like kids just fine," she told him. "As long as they belong to someone else and keep their distance."

He nodded, making no effort to hide his disappointment. "So you can probably sympathize with the woman who left that little bundle of joy on your doorstep, can't you? You'd probably do the same thing if you found yourself saddled with a baby you didn't want."

Claire knew there was little reason to dignify that allegation with a response. But she couldn't quite help herself from retorting, "I would *never* abandon a child. Nor would I conceive one I couldn't care for. So no, I don't sympathize with her. But I do think it's wrong to summarily judge and sentence her without knowing the circumstances of her situation.

"Still," she hurried on before Nick could interrupt, as he clearly wanted to do, "I can see how a guy like *you* would see the situation as either-or. You never were much good at distinguishing shades of gray, were you? It was always Nick's way or no way with you."

She could tell there was more—a lot more—that he wanted to say on that particular matter, but he set his jaw resolutely and instead asked, "What else can you tell me about this episode that might be helpful?"

For the next quarter hour Nick asked a lot of questions

about the baby's abandonment that Claire did her best to answer. For most of them, however, she could provide nothing helpful. Everything had just happened so quickly, and she'd just been so surprised by it all, that few details had registered in her brain.

Finally, though, Nick seemed to run out of questions, so he clicked his pen again, flipped the notebook closed and tucked both back inside his coat pocket. Then he spared another backward glance toward the sleeping baby and turned back to study Claire with clear concern. She waited for him to pose another question about her unexpected visitor. But very softly he asked, "How've you been, Claire?"

The quick and unexpected change of subject—not to mention the unmistakable tenderness in his tone—caught her off guard, as did the glimmer of genuine affection that briefly lit his eyes. Gone, for an instant, was the antagonism and accusation that had heated the air between them earlier. Gone was any sign that he felt anything other than honest curiosity about her well-being. For a moment, Claire had no idea what to say. Because for a moment, she honestly didn't know how she'd been.

"Um, fine," she finally muttered, shaking off the odd sensation that everything in her life was wrong. "I, uh…" She swallowed with some difficulty and glanced away. "I've been fine."

"Just fine?"

She inhaled a shaky breath and released it slowly, wishing she could turn back the clock almost twenty years, to the day she'd first lain eyes on Nick Campisano at Overdale High School in Gloucester City. It really had been a lifetime ago. Back then, Claire had been the shy, skinny new kid, hiding behind big glasses and baggy clothes. Nick Campisano, with his dark good looks and gregarious disposition and total self-confidence, in his red-and-gold, multilettered football jacket, had seemed like a Roman god. Even as a sophomore, he'd already been making a splash on the varsity teams. And Claire, as a lowly freshman, hadn't entered his sphere of existence at all.

No, that hadn't happened until she was a junior, and he was a senior. When she'd gotten contact lenses and gone through a second puberty that had rounded her out nicely. They'd been in study hall together, where fate—and Mrs. Ballantine—had thrown them together at the same table. It had taken all of five minutes for Nick to charm Claire into going out with him. After that, there had been no turning back for either of them.

Not until the day she graduated from Princeton with a BS in biology and an acceptance letter to Yale med school. That was the day everything began to unravel.

"Yes, fine," she told him when she remembered that his question required an answer. "I'm fine," she repeated yet again, as if by saying it often enough, she could make the statement true.

"Yeah, well, I guess I can't disagree," he told her, his voice low and appraising. "You look terrific."

A tiny splash of heat ignited in the pit of her stomach at his carelessly offered observation. Immediately she extinguished it. No sense getting fired up over something that wasn't going to happen, she told herself. Unable to stop herself, however, she replied, "You look pretty good yourself."

He shrugged the compliment off quite literally, then waited until she was gazing at his face again before he continued. "Nice house," he remarked with absolutely no inflection one way or another. "Guess you're doing pretty well these days."

"I do all right," she concurred.

He expelled a single, almost derisive chuckle. "All

right,'' he echoed. ''You probably paid more for this house than I'll make in ten years.''

She couldn't contradict him, because she knew he was right. So she said nothing.

''Guess you got everything you wanted, huh, Claire?''

Well, not quite everything, Nick.

''How would you even know what I wanted?'' she asked softly, without bitterness. She didn't want to return to their earlier acrimony, but she wasn't about to let him get away with thinking that what had happened between them was all her fault. ''You never even bothered to ask.''

His easygoing demeanor quickly vanished, and he went back to being brittle and wary. ''There was a time when you and I wanted the same thing,'' he said. ''I didn't need to ask.''

Although that wasn't quite true, Claire didn't call him on it. She only told him, ''We were kids, Nick. We couldn't possibly know what we wanted then.''

''Hey, speak for yourself,'' he countered. ''I knew exactly what *I* wanted.''

''Then maybe you should have taken better care of it,'' she replied.

Nick studied Claire in the faint, golden light of the very expensive-looking lamp that shone from the other side of the room. And he tried with all his might to make his heart stop pounding against his breastbone the way it was. Nothing had brought him more happiness back then than taking care of Claire Wainwright. Nothing. And he couldn't think of anything that would bring him more joy now.

But there had been other things that were more important to her than Nick Campisano. And for that, more than anything else, he couldn't forgive her. He'd offered to build his entire life around her and the family they would have created together. And for that, she'd dumped him. Because that wouldn't have been enough for her.

God, she looked incredible, though. Better than he could possibly have imagined. Better than she had ever looked before. The last time he'd seen her, he'd been too stunned and overwhelmed to say anything to her. All he'd been able to do was stare at her from across the dance floor of the Knights of Columbus hall, telling himself to ask her to dance, then cursing himself for wanting to.

By now, they should have been celebrating their tenth or twelfth wedding anniversary. They should have had a house full of rug rats crawling and running all over the place. They should have been worrying about carpooling and school plays and orthodontists and how old Nick, Jr. should be before they'd let him get a golden retriever.

They should have been a family, a great, big, boisterous—and very happy—South Jersey family. Instead, they were both alone. And speaking for himself, happiness—real, honest, genuine happiness—was one thing he'd never quite been able to find.

"I listened to you, Claire," he defended himself softly. "I just didn't think you meant what you said. I couldn't believe you'd think there were other things that were more important than us."

Her lips parted in what was obvious surprise, but she said nothing, neither to deny, nor to confirm, his allegations. Instead, she only wrapped her arms around herself more tightly, as if she were trying to keep herself from falling apart.

"So, um, what are you going to do about the baby?" she finally asked.

He told himself he was relieved by her question, was glad she was no more willing to revisit the past than he was. Somehow, though, the change of subject didn't sit well with him. As it had been for so many years, things just didn't seem settled between the two of them.

"To be honest," he said, "I'm not sure. I should call Social Services, but there was no answer there earlier, so I'm not too hopeful that there's going to be anybody there now. And even if there is, with the weather being the way it is, I don't think there's much chance that anyone's going to want to venture out here tonight."

Claire went pale at his assessment of the situation. "But…but…someone has to make it out here tonight," she said, clearly anxious.

Nick shrugged noncommittally. "Yeah, well, I'll give it my best shot, but don't get your hopes up."

"But someone has to."

"Claire, I—"

"They *have* to, Nick," she interrupted, her tone of voice bordering on panicked.

Nick grew puzzled at her reaction. Hey, he knew Claire was no fan of kids—of course, that was something he didn't find out until the day she'd told him to take a hike—but her reaction now was still kind of surprising. It was just a baby, he thought. What was the big deal?

"I'll make the call," he assured her. "But in this weather, on New Year's Eve, no less, I just wouldn't count on seeing anybody anytime soon. It'd take a miracle to get someone out here tonight."

"Then get me a miracle," she insisted. "Now."

"Why? What's the big deal?"

She expelled one single, incredulous chuckle. "Because I can't take care of this baby by myself," she told him. "There's no way."

He smiled, feeling something warm and totally uncalled-for unwinding in his belly. "Hey, don't sweat it. Even if we can't get anybody from Social Services out here tonight, you won't be by yourself.''

She eyed him curiously. ''I won't?''

''Nah,'' he assured her. ''I'll be glad to stay here to help you out. Any way I can. All night long.''

Three

Just as Nick had suspected, no one answered the phone at Social Services. Nor was there anyone available at any of the other half-dozen numbers he called in an effort to get someone out to the house, to take the baby off Claire's hands. The holiday and the snow had sent every available body out to see to situations that were infinitely more pressing than an abandoned baby who was, at the moment, safe and warm, and in the care of both a government official and a medical doctor.

A disenchanted government official and a very anxious medical doctor, yeah, but still...

Nick settled the cordless phone back into its resting place on the kitchen counter and turned to Claire with a shrug. "Sorry," he said. For some reason, though, he didn't exactly *feel* sorry. There was just something about this situation that prevented him from becoming too overwrought. "But that was the last person I knew to call. Looks like it's going to be tomorrow afternoon at the earliest before anybody can take Sleeping Beauty off your hands.''

They'd moved both baby and basket into the kitchen with them, and now the infant was slumbering peacefully in the middle of the expansive kitchen table—which Nick couldn't help but notice was quite a bit larger than one person could possibly need. By the soft, pink light of a small, terra-cotta lamp that burned atop the—really big—refrigerator, Claire had made a pot of coffee. While he was on the phone, she had filled a mug for each of them, and now she was clutching hers with a brutal grip, as if it were her last handhold on reality.

As if reading his mind, she muttered ''This can't be happening. This has got to be a dream. No, a nightmare,'' she hastily corrected herself. ''I can't believe I'm going to be stuck here with you and a baby until tomorrow afternoon.''

Nick told himself not to take her sentiment to heart, that she was speaking out of panic and fear and nothing more. But it stung to realize that Claire considered spending any amount of time with him and a baby a nightmare. It wasn't exactly surprising, but it did sting.

''Yeah, well, look at it this way,'' he told her, biting back the bitterness that began to pool in his belly again. ''Maybe it won't be until tomorrow afternoon.''

She arched her eyebrows hopefully. ''No?''

He shook his head slowly. Then, gritting his teeth mildly, he told her, ''No. The way things are going, it might very well be the day after.''

This time her eyebrows shot down in an angry V. ''That's not funny.''

He bit back a disgruntled chuckle. ''Tell me about it. If you think I'm any happier to be stranded in close quarters with you than you are to be here with me, think again. I'm the one who got dumped, in case you've forgotten.'' *The one who never stopped loving you,* he added to himself, none too happy about that realization, either.

Why deny it, though? he asked himself. It had been more than a decade since he'd asked Claire to marry him. More than a decade for him to put his feelings for her in the past and move on with his life. And in that length of time, he'd done neither. He still loved her. His love for her had been what prevented him from marrying anyone else. He couldn't, in good conscience, join himself to another woman and devote his life to her, when what he felt for her would only be shade of the love he still harbored for Claire.

And, simply put, he would never love another woman. Not completely. Not the way he had loved Claire. Not as long as Claire still walked the earth, anyway.

He wasn't so bitter that he blamed her for the unhappiness he felt these days. Sure, he'd wanted to be married with kids by now, and his life would never feel complete without a family of his own. But it was his choice to remain single and childless. His choice not to get involved with other women beyond a superficial, physical relationship. His choice to look down the road at the future and see nothing but a solitary existence. He certainly didn't blame Claire for those things. But he didn't exactly forgive her, either.

She sighed fitfully, bringing his thoughts back to the present. "Let's not start this again," she said quietly. "It's pointless. It'll just make this situation that much more difficult to weather. We're not going to learn anything more than we already know about each other."

"Pointless," he echoed hollowly. "Yeah, that's a good word for it," he concurred further. "We have a whole history that was pretty much pointless, don't we?"

"Nick..." she said, her voice tinted with an unmistakable warning.

He lifted both hands and held them palm out, in a gesture of surrender. "Okay, okay," he relented. "I promise to be a good boy. Really, I do."

Claire rolled her eyes, but refrained from comment. Instead, she turned her attention to her new infant centerpiece. "She sure seems to be sleeping a lot. Is that safe? I mean, I thought babies slept really badly."

Nick shrugged, gazing in that direction himself. "Depends on the baby," he said. "A lot of them are lousy sleepers. But some of them sleep like rocks. Besides, this one's gotta be at least six or seven months old. By now she should be sleeping fairly well at night. And, hey," he added softly, "tonight hasn't exactly been conducive to good sleep for her, has it?"

Claire turned and eyed him suspiciously through lowered lids. Very coolly, she remarked, "You seem to know an awful lot about babies. Do you...have one or two of your own?"

He couldn't help noting that she glanced quickly down at his—ringless—left hand as she made the comment. *Ooo,* he thought. *Touchy. Is that jealousy tinting Claire's voice now? Well, well, well.*

He shook his head. "No, I'm not married with kids. But I've got a lot of nieces and nephews. Angie had twins a month ago, bringing her own personal contribution to four, and—"

"You're kidding!" Claire exclaimed happily. "Angie? Little Angie has four kids?"

Her smile was dazzling, her delight infectious, and Nick couldn't help but smile, too. "Hey, 'little Angie' is twenty-eight years old," he pointed out. "She's been married for six years now."

Claire shook her head in disbelief. "That's so amazing," she said. "I remember her tagging along after us when she was just a kid."

"She always liked you a lot," he told her. "She wouldn't speak to me for months after we broke up. She was sure I did or said something to you that made you run off to Connecticut."

"Nick..." Claire said again, again with clear warning.

"I'm not trying to rehash old business," he told her honestly. "I'm just stating a fact is all. You can't expect us to spend any amount of time together and not bring up some part of the past." He covered the distance necessary to bring him within arm's length of her. And with no small effort, he refrained from reaching out to touch her. "We were a big part of each other's lives once upon a time, whether you like to admit that or not."

Her lips parted fractionally in surprise at his charge. For a long moment, she only gazed up at his face, her cobalt eyes deep and compelling and filled with some emotion he was probably better off not trying to figure out. Claire's eyes had always been his undoing, he recalled now, too late. So blue. So arresting. So damned expressive. She could never hide her feelings, because invariably her eyes had betrayed her. They'd always been her own undoing, too.

And right now her eyes were telling Nick that she was remembering those times even better than he remembered them himself. Every muscle and microbe, every sense and sensibility he possessed screamed at him to reach out to her. To take her in his arms and pull her close. To relive those moments of the past and create a few more for the future. Even after more than a decade of separation, even after the emotional wringing he'd suffered as a result of her abandonment, he still wanted Claire. With all his heart, with all his soul. Till death do them part.

Great, Nick. This is just great.

"It's not that I don't want to admit how important we used to be to each other," she said, scattering his thoughts, but doing nothing to alleviate the jumble of his emotions. "On the contrary," she added quietly, "maybe I remember that part of it better than you do."

Nodding slowly, but unwilling to reveal just how much her statement shook him, he asked, "Then what is it? What's wrong?"

She sighed again, opened her mouth to say something, then shut it without uttering a word. She only shook her head silently and spun around, but not before Nick caught the shimmer of tears in her eyes. Something twisted tight in his gut at the sight.

Yeah, those eyes, he thought again. They'd always been trouble. Looked like some things, at least, hadn't changed a bit.

Claire couldn't imagine what had come over her to make her act this way. As if it wasn't already bad enough that she'd be responsible—at least in part—for an abandoned baby for another day, perhaps two. As if it wasn't already bad enough that the person with whom she was sharing that responsibility was a man she'd once banished from her life, a man she'd never expected to see again, in anything other than passing. As if it wasn't already bad enough that the two of them were traveling down a memory lane that was pockmarked with land mines that might go off at any second.

No, as if all that wasn't already bad enough, she was beginning to think that maybe, just maybe, way down deep inside, in a distant, lonely place she'd thought locked away forever, she was still in love with Nick Campisano. Even after all these years. Even after the emotional upheaval she'd somehow managed to survive upon their parting. Even after all that, she sensed that there was still a part of herself—a rather large part, evidently—that wanted Nick in her life. Substantially. Eternally.

Wonderful, Claire. You've just ascended to the next level of stupidity.

She spread one hand open over her eyes, pretending to swipe away fatigue, praying that Nick hadn't noticed the presence of tears. Why on earth was she crying? she wondered. She was just exhausted, she tried to reassure herself. It was almost three o'clock in the morning, and she'd been up for nearly twenty-four hours straight. Even before that she'd been tired. She'd never been a good sleeper. The holiday season always made that worse. And the emotional stress of the last few hours had helped not at all.

Tired, she echoed to herself. Weary. Fatigued. That was why she was experiencing this strange wave of melancholy memory. It was nothing more than that. She couldn't possibly still be in love with Nick after all this time. It made no sense.

Oh, really? a little voice inside her piped up. *Then why have you never been able to make a commitment to another man? Why have you never found anyone who made you feel the way Nick made you feel? Why is he the yardstick by which you measure every potential mate?*

Instead of answering the little voice, Claire commanded it in no uncertain terms to just shut up and leave her alone because it had no idea what it was yammering about, anyway.

Dragging her hand over her face one final time, Claire spun back around to face Nick. He looked as exhausted and dejected as she did. They both obviously needed sleep—

and lots of it. She spared a glance for the solidly sleeping infant and told herself they should take advantage of this brief reprieve. No telling when the baby would awaken again, or how long it would be before she went to sleep after that. Even an hour or two of rest would help enormously.

"We should go to bed," she said.

At the soft sound of disbelief Nick uttered, she closed her eyes. "That's not what I meant and you know it," she said flatly, turning to face him again. When she opened her eyes, she saw that he didn't look quite as tired as he had before. No, in fact, he appeared quite capable of staying awake for hours, if offered the right kind of incentive.

"Hey, I don't know jack," he told her. "Why? What were *you* talking about? My, my, my, Claire. Get your mind out of the gutter."

"Yeah, you wish it was in the gutter," she shot back. But somehow she couldn't quite quell the soft smile that threatened to bloom.

Nick smiled, too, though his own effort was considerably more predatory. "I remember a few occasions when we both had our minds there. It was a lot of fun. To put it mildly."

Claire's smile fell at his willingness to continue with what she considered a very dangerous topic. But she couldn't battle the heat seeping through her at the memories—anything *but* mild—that exploded fast and furious in her brain. Fast and furious. That was how it had always been between them. As if they both feared they'd never get enough of each other. As if they'd somehow known their time together was limited, and they had to make the most of every second. As if they couldn't bear to be apart. As if they needed to consume each other in order to survive.

We were both kids then, she tried to remind herself. *It was nothing more than hormones.*

That was all it had been to make them react to each other with the instant and complete intensity that they had, she told herself again. Hormones. Biology. Chemistry. And okay, anatomy, too. It was all very scientific, very natural. A chemical reaction, nothing more. A really, really *hot* chemical reaction, granted, but a reaction nonetheless. They were two mature adults now, fully capable of keeping that kind of response under control. No way would they burn for each other the way they once had.

She gazed at Nick again, feeling her maturity level drop as quickly as her temperature rose. Uh-oh.

"It's over," she told him, trying not to choke on the lie. "That's all in the past. There's nothing there between us now."

He emitted another, louder, sound of disbelief in response to her statement. "Right," he said, not bothering to hide his sarcasm. "Sure, Claire. Whatever you say. If it makes you feel better, then by all means, you go ahead and wallow in your little fantasy."

"It's not a fantasy," she insisted. "It's true."

He eyed her levelly as he took a step toward her. "So you've put the past completely behind you. Is that what you're telling me?"

She nodded and somehow managed to murmur, "Yes."

He took another casual step forward. "Since opening that door a couple hours ago, you haven't experienced a single stir of old emotion?"

This time she shook her head, but her voice was a little shaky as she told him, "No."

Another, less casual, step forward. "Not even one little spark of heat?"

This time Claire didn't trust her voice not to betray her, so she only shook her head again and remained silent.

Nick, however, continued to speak. And take yet another step toward her. "Not so much as a banked ember?"

This time Claire couldn't even manage to shake her head. All she could do was watch Nick's face, noting the flicker of heat and the play of light in his dark eyes as he drew nearer still.

"So then it's just me," he continued, his voice dropping to a dangerously low pitch. "It's just me who's been feeling this current of electricity jumping back and forth between us like a generator wound way too tight?"

She cleared her throat with some difficulty and forced herself to respond. Unfortunately, the only response that emerged was lame at best. "I, uh…I think you must be imagining things, Nick."

One more step forward, and he stood immediately in front of her, with scarcely a breath of air separating them. She told herself she should be offended that he'd usurped her space the way he had, without asking her permission, without thought for how it might make her feel. It was just another reminder of why the two of them hadn't worked out together the first time around.

As much as she had loved him, Nick had always overrun Claire. He hadn't meant to do it, and it hadn't been because he'd wanted more than she was willing to give. That's just the way Nick was. Overwhelming. Larger than life. Too big, too happy, too outgoing, too gregarious, too loving, too…too…

Too *too*.

Claire had always felt overshadowed, overpowered. Not just by Nick, but by the entire Campisano clan. They'd all been just like him. Too affectionate, too kind, too nurturing. All of them had always been totally in tune with one another, as if they were all different parts of one big, beautifully purring machine. Where one lacked, the other supplied. Where one hurt, the other healed. Where one despaired, the other encouraged.

And Claire, who had never been witness to such a thing in her own family, whose too-few relatives had been cautious about showing any kind of emotion at all, had felt like a complete outsider when she was among the Campisanos. As much as she'd loved and needed Nick, and as much as she had cared for his family, she'd just never felt like she would belong with them the way he so naturally did.

And she'd known that such closeness and intimacy was what Nick would demand in any family the two of them might start together. He'd made that crystal clear. He'd wanted them to have a half-dozen kids, just as his folks had done. He'd wanted them to live in the old neighborhood where his parents lived, had wanted Claire to stay at home with the kids, had wanted to work himself to death to take care of the family financially. He'd wanted to be the kind of father his dad had been—one who came home at night and on the weekends, and gathered up the brood for a rousing round of horsy, or an extended game of ball.

He'd wanted their family to be just like his family. Campisanos: The Next Generation. And Claire just couldn't see that happening. She hadn't wanted to give birth to and care for six children—or even one child. She hadn't wanted to be a homemaker—she'd wanted to be a doctor, as her parents had been. She just hadn't envisioned her life with Nick in the same way he had planned it at all.

She simply wasn't a family person. She wasn't built that way. As much as she may have wished that she was. And Nick had just never understood that about her.

And now, as he stood before her, gazing down at her the

way he had gazed down at her all those years ago, she felt those same sensations of disassociation warring with her desire—her need—to fit in. At the moment, however, it wasn't the Campisano family with whom she wanted to fit herself. It was Nick alone. And she wanted to fit with him exactly the way she had before.

He seemed to sense her conflicting responses, because he didn't push her any further. Well, not much further. He only lifted a hand to her hair, twining one shoulder-length tress around his index finger, winding it loosely, slowly, until his palm was flush with her jaw. Then, after only a small hesitation, he cupped her chin in his hand and tilted her head back, so that he could look fully upon her face and into her eyes.

"You can't lie to me, Claire," he said softly, almost painfully. "You never could, you know. Even when you told me you didn't want to marry me, I knew you were lying. I knew you wanted to. But you said no anyway. And I just couldn't figure out why."

She opened her mouth to reply, then realized she had no idea what to say. His simple touch had jumbled her thoughts, incited her emotions, stimulated her entire body. A faint ribbon of heat wound through her, puddling in her midsection before easing out to every cell she possessed. Instinctively Claire tilted her head to the side, into his hand, into his touch, as easily and naturally as a petal would turn toward the sun. She closed her eyes, telling herself it would only be for an instant, just long enough to give herself a glimpse of what might have been.

Too late, she realized that a glimpse, an instant, would never be enough. That even a glimpse, even an instant, would rouse too many emotions she'd thought long buried.

Nick seemed to feel that way, too, because he took a small step backward, as if her reaction had startled him somehow, had put him on alert. He didn't, however, re-move his hand, and continued to reach out to her, as if he were more afraid of letting her go. Not knowing why she did it, Claire took a step forward, circling his wrist with her own hand. And then, surprising herself as much as she did Nick, she turned her head more and settled a chaste kiss at the center of his palm.

"Why—why did you do that?" he stammered.

And all Claire could think to say in response was, "For old times' sake."

His mouth dropped open in clear surprise, and had the moment not been so poignantly painful, she might have laughed at his expression. She couldn't recall ever getting the drop on Nick Campisano. Now, after all these years, she'd finally managed to leave him speechless.

She only wished now that she could understand why she had even tried.

He opened his mouth to reply, but no words emerged. Not because he had nothing to say, but because the little bundle of joy who had arrived on the doorstep some hours ago chose that minute to awaken. The soft sounds the baby made while rousing to consciousness twisted something in-side Claire she'd never felt before. Dammit, why couldn't the kid wake up screaming and irritable? Why did she have to sound so...so sweet?

Not surprisingly, Nick was the one who responded to the baby's summons, but there was a slight hesitation on his part before he did so. With one final, cryptic, glance at Claire, he crossed the kitchen to the table, scooping the baby out of the basket and into his arms. The moment he did so, the soft sounds of waking increased, and Claire braced herself for the inevitable howling of earlier to return. But no such eruption occurred. Instead, when she turned around, she saw Nick cradling the baby in his arms, smiling as the infant clutched his nose in one chubby fist.

"I love it when they do that," he said, his voice warmed by his laughter. "Like they've never seen a nose before and can't imagine what it's for."

The baby cooed and squeezed harder, then released Nick's nose and began to squirm.

"Uh-oh," he said.

Claire's mental alarms went off with a deafening crash. "What?" she asked anxiously. "What's wrong with her? Is she okay?"

"Prepare yourself," he told her, his voice deadly serious. He was still looking at the baby, his attention totally concentrated on its face.

Claire grew more frantic. "What?" she demanded. "What is it?"

But still he eyed the baby with much scrutiny. "I think this is going to get ugly," he said.

"Nick!" she cried, rushing over to the table. The baby's face was nearly purple, its eyes squinched shut tight, its little mouth screwed up in what looked like pain.

"My God!" Claire exclaimed. "What's wrong with her?"

However, Nick seemed to be not at all concerned. "Give it a minute," he said.

The baby began to make a gurgling sound that Claire likened to choking. "For God's sake, do the Heimlich Maneuver on her!" she said. When he still made no move to attend to the baby's condition, she punched him on the arm and added, "Nick! Do something!"

"Hey, I don't have to do something," he said, chuckling again. "Feels like she's doing enough for all of us."

Claire opened her mouth to object again, but she was

overcome by *such* a smell…one that just about knocked her over. Whew. That was really bad. Really, *really* bad.

"My God," she repeated, with less alarm this time. She realized now why Nick hadn't been more alarmed. Though the aroma that surrounded them now was pretty doggone alarming. She pinched her nose closed with two fingers. "What has her mother been feeding her? Chimichangas?"

Nick laughed harder, the sound a mixture of both delight and relief, and the tension of a few moments ago evaporated. Here Claire had thought the baby was suffering from some heinous illness, when in fact Baby Girl Doe had simply taken it upon herself to just do what comes naturally.

"I am *not* going to change that diaper," Claire stated quite adamantly.

His laughter subsided, but a warm, wonderful, wicked smile still hovered about his mouth. "Why not?" he asked innocently.

She pinched her fingers more tightly over her nose. "Because it's clearly radioactive."

Nick laughed again, and it was obvious that he, like she, was making light of the situation more because they wanted to alleviate the awkward emotions that had risen between them, than it was because of the symbolism of the baby's timing.

"I'll change her this time," he said. "But we're in this together, Claire. Next time you get diaper duty."

She released her nose, then wrinkled it in disgust. "Oh, goody," she muttered. "I can't wait."

Yet another reason to avoid motherhood, she told herself. Somehow, though, the argument wasn't as successful in convincing her as she had hoped it would be. Even after releasing her nose to fill her nostrils with the…pungent… aroma of baby doo-doo, Claire couldn't quite work up the revulsion she wanted to feel.

Oh, well, she thought. They still had a night—and day—ahead of them. There were bound to be plenty of opportunities for her to discover what lousy mother material she was. Surely by tomorrow evening all three of them would realize what a farce it would be to think otherwise.

Surely.

Four

Fifteen minutes later, with the baby's nuclear fusion tank empty, so to speak, Nick settled her—in a clean diaper—onto his lap, to refuel. The moment he touched the bottle to her little bow-shaped mouth, she latched on to the rubber nipple and sucked hungrily, curling fat little fingers around his wrist as she did so. And just like that, he melted a bit inside.

Man, he loved babies. He loved kids even more. He was a total pushover where his nieces and nephews were concerned, and every single one of those little con artists knew it. Need a new bike? Hey, ask Uncle Nick. Need somebody to take you to the Phillies game next weekend? Yo, ask Uncle Nick. Need somebody to do your math homework for you? Eh, ask Uncle Nick. Uh, except about logarithms—he don't know jack there.

Yeah, Uncle Nick was a complete softy when it came to the kids. Everybody in the Campisano clan knew it. Yet,

he was the only member of the family who hadn't repro-
duced.

Then again, he was the only member of the family who'd
fallen in love with somebody who didn't *want* to reproduce.
Which was something he'd never been able to understand
about Claire. Ever since he'd met her, he'd thought she'd
make a great mom. She had all the necessary traits. She
was loving and good, and kind and sweet. She had patience,
but she didn't put up with any guff from anybody. And
okay, so maybe she had trouble showing her affection
sometimes, well... Nobody was perfect. That was something she'd be more comfortable with as time went by.

And as for her hips... Well, say no more.

The thought brought his glance up from the baby in his
lap, to settle his gaze on that part of her anatomy. He found
Claire standing on the other side of the kitchen, her arms
wrapped around herself again in that defensive pose. Great
hips, he couldn't help but note. And not just great for bear-
ing children, either. They were nice just for looking at.
Lush, curvy, perfect for both cradling life and the fit of a
man's hands.

Now, if he could just do something about that taut disposition of hers....

When they first started dating, Nick had thought Claire
was one uptight individual, and he'd looked forward to
loosening her up. In spite of his enthusiasm, however, she'd
fought off his efforts for months. She'd oh-so-casually
shrug off his arm whenever he draped it around her shoulders. She'd find excuses to release his hand whenever he
wove his fingers with hers. For the first few months they
spent together, she'd always been the one who ended the
kiss, the one who pulled out of an embrace.

For a long time, he'd thought maybe she just didn't like
him as much as he liked her. Gradually, though, he'd come

to understand that Claire's resistance to displaying emotion wasn't the result of any lack of feeling on her part. On the contrary, he'd ultimately realized that she felt things more deeply than most people did. But she'd never had the opportunity to show anyone she cared about that she did indeed care about them. Her parents had been nice people, but they hadn't been demonstrative people. They'd obviously loved Claire, but they'd never voiced that love in so many words, had never shown that love with affectionate touches. And because of that, Claire, too, had always had difficulty revealing any honest emotion.

Frankly, Nick couldn't understand that kind of behavior at all. Campisano code dictated that if you loved somebody, you told them. You showed them. You let them know how much in as many ways possible, every chance you got. Hey, life was too short to spend it pussyfooting around the truth. What good did it do to pretend? What was the big deal about letting someone know how you felt about them? What was the point of hiding all that inside? But the Wainwrights just hadn't been the kind of people to offer physical—or even verbal—displays of affection. Even though Claire was obviously the kind of person who craved them.

And that was where the really confusing part came in. Once she'd gotten used to him, used to his way of doing things, Claire had never turned away from Nick. She'd curled into his big body whenever he wanted to hold her. Their hands had always found their way to joining, as if by mutual consent. Their lovemaking had always been intense and uninhibited. There had been times when he thought maybe that was the main reason she loved him so much—because he was the first person in her life who'd made his feelings for her clear.

But something had gone wrong somewhere. Claire had chosen her independence over him. And he still couldn't quite understand why. He had thought she was happy being with him. He had thought she loved his family. He had thought she wanted to be with him forever.

In many ways he still thought that.

But she seemed to be as unwilling to explore her feelings now as she had been back then. She seemed to be as resistant to even discussing a possible future with him now as she had been a decade ago. Yet, somehow he got the impression that, even though she was living her life exactly the way she had chosen to live it, Claire wasn't quite fulfilled or happy these days. There still seemed to be something missing for her. Something very important. Maybe something that she couldn't even identify, if asked to do so.

Thing was, though, he thought further, heartening, they had hours trapped together here in her house to explore whatever that something might be.

Well, well, well. Sometimes life worked right, he thought. Ever the optimist, that was Nick Campisano. And he sure wasn't going to turn down an opportunity like this one. Fate wasn't something he put a lot of stock in. And destiny, as far as he was concerned, was one of those concepts best left for a Yanni CD. Still, it was awfully interesting how their paths had crossed again on a night like New Year's Eve—rife for reminiscing and planning for the future—and because of something like an abandoned baby. It was awfully convenient that the two of them would be trapped together for hours, faced with memories of an unsettled past and the responsibility for a child whose future was entirely uncertain.

"Should we feed her some of the baby food in the jars?" Claire asked as Nick watched her, oblivious to the workings of his brain. Her gaze, however, was focused not on him, but on the infant in his lap.

He shrugged. "It's probably not necessary until morning."

She eyed the clock. "I hate to tell you this, Nick. But it *is* morning."

"I mean real morning," he told her. "Normal morning. If her mother is as conscientious as you seem to think she is—oh, except for that part about abandoning her baby in a snowstorm, I mean," he couldn't keep himself from adding, much to Claire's obvious consternation, "then the formula should tide her over for a few more hours. She'll probably go to sleep again. At least, she should. Let's see if this, and maybe a little rocking, will be enough to put her back down."

"There's a rocking chair up in my bedroom," she said. "I'd offer to go up and get it and bring it down here, but it's too big to move."

The baby sucked down the last of the formula, and after placing the empty bottle on the table, Nick hefted her onto his shoulder—over which he'd placed a clean dish towel, just in case—for a burp. "No problem," he said. "I can take her up there and rock her. If you bring the basket up, she can just sleep in your room."

The expression that crossed Claire's face at his suggestion bordered on panic. "In my room?" she echoed. "You're going to put her in *my* room?"

"Sure," he said. "Why not? That way you could get some sleep, too."

"And what about you?"

"With digs this big?" he replied, rubbing a hand gently over the baby's back in the hopes of conjuring a nice burp. "Something tells me you have a spare room up there somewhere."

She nodded. "A couple of them. So why don't you take

the baby's basket into one of them and let her sleep with *you?* You know more about her than *I* do.''

''But the rocking chair is in *your* room,'' he reminded her. ''And hey, what better way for you to learn about this stuff, huh?'' he added with a smile, mainly because he knew it would get her riled. And he'd much rather see Claire riled than panicked, the way she was now.

''I don't want to learn about this stuff,'' she said through gritted teeth. ''That's the whole point. You always wanted to forget that part, didn't you?''

''Hey, you never brought that part up, until I mentioned it.'' Somehow he couldn't keep himself from adding, ''Remember? It was that day I asked you to marry me, and you threw my proposal right back in my face.''

She dropped her fisted hands to her hips, an action that caused her robe to fall open over her tailored pajamas, and her pajama top to gape just the slightest bit at the neck. Just enough to reveal a hint of the dusky valley between her breasts. Just enough to make Nick's blood go rocketing through his system when he recalled—too well—that once-beloved territory.

''That's it,'' she said in clipped tones. ''We're obviously not going to be able to avoid talking about that, so let's just get it out in the clear right now.''

Oh, yeah. She was riled all right. Direct hit. Score one for the Campisano kid.

''Shhh,'' he murmured, more to keep her from rushing him with both fists flying than because he sensed that the baby was falling asleep. ''I think she's going down.''

Claire eyed him venomously.

''Where did you say that rocking chair is?'' he asked, lowering his voice even more.

Her mouth flattened into a tight line, but she was clearly

uncertain of his motives. "Up in my bedroom," she told him almost grudgingly.

"Which is where?"

"Upstairs," she muttered. After releasing a long, put-upon sigh, she added, "Follow me."

Anywhere, he thought.

He rose carefully with the squirming baby, waited for Claire to retrieve the basket from the table, then followed her back through the hallway and living room to the wide sweeping staircase near the front door. He still couldn't get over the size of this house, the luxuriousness of its furnishings. Claire must be making money hand over fist these days.

He'd known from the time he first met her that she wanted to be a doctor someday, like her folks. But he had never honestly given much thought to the potential reality of that. Mainly because, as the two of them grew closer and spent more time together, he honestly hadn't thought she'd go through with her studies beyond college. He'd just been so sure she'd be so much happier as a wife and mother—*his* wife, and the mother of *his* kids. But she was clearly hugely successful in her work, he realized now, and it was obviously something to which she'd devoted her entire life.

At least, he hoped it was her work to which she devoted her entire life. Somehow he couldn't quite banish—or tolerate—the knowledge that she might possibly be sharing all this, sharing her whole life, with someone else.

Her life, he thought again. The life he'd wanted her to devote to him and their family instead. It should have been *their* life.

Okay, so maybe he shouldn't have expected her to be something other than what she claimed to want to be herself, he conceded reluctantly. Maybe he shouldn't have assumed she would adopt a role he created for her. Maybe he should have taken her insistence on having a career more seriously. Maybe he should have paid better attention when she'd cut off all his chatter about the six kids and the brick Cape Cod they'd buy in Gloucester City, right up the street from his parents. Maybe he should have listened a little more closely when she'd expressed her own needs and desires to do something else. He'd just figured that, deep down, her needs and desires had mirrored his own. So maybe back then he'd been, you know...

Wrong.

There. He'd admitted it. Maybe he'd been...wrong...all those years ago to assume that Claire would want the same things for the future that he wanted for them. Maybe he'd been...wrong...in suggesting that she conform to a lifestyle he alone envisioned for the two of them. Maybe he'd been...wrong...not to take her insistence to the contrary more seriously. Maybe he'd been...wrong...about a lot of things.

And on the heels of that, he wondered if maybe there was time to make amends. Time to make things, you know...

Right.

Claire's bedroom, when he entered it, was decorated like a harem—he couldn't think of any other way to describe it. It was just all filmy and soft and light and pretty. Totally plush, totally posh, totally sumptuous, totally feminine.

The rug spanning the hardwood floor was an intricate piece of floral artwork, executed in muted pastels of blue and peach and ivory. The bed wasn't quite a canopy number, but it had a...a...a round thing...hanging from the ceiling, from which long, sheer curtains of ivory, pale blue and peach descended, caught on each of the four posters and tied with color-coordinated ribbon. The bedspread, too, was a blue that was softer than the sky, made of silk, if Nick wasn't mistaken. Fat, tasseled pillows of varying shapes, sizes and soft colors were scattered about, on the floor and the bed, on a club chair and a…a…a whatcha-macallit. A chaise thing. Or something like that.

He wasn't surprised. Claire had always been a sensualist, big on touching *things,* if not people. It made sense that she would surround herself with beauty and texture, and sleep under something soft, silky and seductive. He just wished she'd sleep under—

Oops. His thoughts were getting away from him again. Forcing his mind—and libido—back to the matter at hand, he noted the rest of the furnishings—all of them rich, over-stuffed, pale blue and peach in color, and very expensive looking—until he located an upholstered rocking chair in the corner. He made his way in that direction while Claire settled the baby's basket on the floor by the bed. And he pretended not to notice the frilly, girly fabric that covered the rocker as he sat down on it.

Claire spoke not a word as he made himself comfortable and laid a hand on the baby's back, but she glanced away when he started to croon softly in the baby's ear. Naturally, having the Jersey boy link in common, Bruce Springsteen had always been a favorite of Nick's, so he chose a softer, less raucous rendition of "No Surrender" to help put the baby to sleep. As it did with his nieces and nephews, the song worked beautifully. Within minutes, the infant was fast asleep again.

Nick stood and very carefully placed the baby back in her basket, then turned his attention immediately to Claire. She was gazing down at the infant with a look of mild curiosity warming her features, as if she wasn't quite sure what to make of the sleeping baby, but was somehow drawn to it nonetheless. And as he watched that expression bloom upon her face, something inside Nick stirred hopefully. Maybe, just maybe…

"Interesting choice of lullaby," she said quietly, scattering his thoughts.

He shrugged noncommittally. "I just like that song," he replied, just as softly.

She nodded slowly. "Funny you should choose something that was popular when we were kids."

"Is it?" he asked mildly.

"And funny that it should be a song about aging and giving up the past, and leaving it behind, so that those who are young now can enjoy it."

Again, he murmured, "Is it?"

Claire glanced up and eyed him levelly. "Yes. It is. Feeling your mortality, Nick?"

He shook his head. "Not my mortality, no."

"Then what?"

He shrugged again. "Hey, like I said, I just like the song."

"Mmm."

He offered no comment to her quiet concession, probably because he wasn't sure what to say. He only gazed at her in silence, noting a few threads of silver in her jet hair, the faint fan of lines surrounding her blue, blue eyes and bracketing her red, red mouth. And he couldn't help thinking that she looked better now than she had back then, and here they were standing in her bedroom in the middle of the night, and God, he wanted to pull her close and bury himself in her softness and warmth, and never let her go forever and ever and ever.

When he didn't answer her, she mimicked his earlier gesture from downstairs, tipping her head toward the door, indicating he should follow her out of the room, where they could talk without fear of waking the baby. He extended a hand in silent indication for her to precede him, and she made her way across the hall, to a room immediately opposite hers.

When she flicked on a dresser top lamp, Nick saw that they had entered a spare bedroom furnished just as sumptuously and sensuously as Claire's own was. But where hers had been impossibly feminine, this one was decidedly more masculine, and he couldn't help but wonder if she had a regular—male—guest who occupied the room.

The colors were stronger, the furniture larger and sturdier. But as had been the case with Claire's bedroom, the unmistakable feel of wealth was present here. The dark green walls and jewel-toned Oriental rug were the focal points, along with the massive sleigh bed and armoire crafted of gleaming mahogany. Once again, Nick was struck by how much Claire was worth these days, what a huge success she'd made of herself in her chosen career. And he told himself it didn't intimidate him at all.

It didn't. Really. It just…you know…gave him pause. Or something.

She started talking first, keeping her voice low and level, despite the fact that the baby was a full room and hallway away, with the door pulled closed, and couldn't possibly hear what they were saying. But as he watched her face, he realized the reason her voice was low and level *wasn't* because she feared waking the baby. It was because she just barely managed to keep her emotions in check.

She was still obviously pretty mad about the discussion they had begun in the kitchen a few moments ago, the one they had left unfinished in order to get the baby sleeping again. Looked like it wasn't going to remain unfinished for long, Nick thought.

"I guess we should have settled this twelve years ago," she began, "because there's never been a real feeling of completion between you and me, has there? We never did really end it fully, completely, the way we should have. I thought we did, but it's obvious that there's still a lot you want to say to me. And maybe there's a lot I still want to say to you, too.''

He couldn't disagree with her. Not completely, anyway. Like Claire, he was by no means convinced that they had ended things twelve years ago. On each of the handful of occasions when they'd run into each other over the ensuing years, there had been an unmistakable and immediate awareness between them, a feeling that time had dissolved away, and they'd never really been apart. A feeling that they might very well pick up where they had left off, and go back to being madly, passionately, irretrievably in love.

Deep down, Nick couldn't help wondering if maybe that was the reason he had remained single all this time. Because he'd never quite been able to shake the feeling that there was still hope for him and Claire to work things out. That things weren't really over between them. That they could indeed pick up where they had left off, and go back to being in love.

Yeah, right, he thought derisively, noting the blaze of combat that flickered in her eyes. The way she was looking at him now, he'd be better off spontaneously combusting. No woman could look at a man like that if she was interested in salvaging something of what they'd had together more than a decade ago. Then again, he thought further, the fact that she felt so strongly about him—even if that feeling wasn't exactly love or devotion—might just be a good sign.

It was a thin line…and all that jazz.

''Should we have ended it more fully and completely back then?'' he asked. ''*Could* we have ended it more fully and completely? I mean, think about it, Claire. Was it even *possible* for us to end it twelve years ago? Is it possible to do it now? Do you really think there will ever be a time when you and I don't respond to each other in some deeply elemental way?''

She took a step backward at his vehemence, and her lips parted fractionally in clear surprise. Nick hadn't meant to just spill his feelings that way, but what was the point of denying it? He honestly didn't think they *could* end completely the relationship they'd once had. What the two of them had generated would burn forever. There was no way to extinguish it. It would be like trying to put out a tire fire.

And wasn't that just the perfect blue-collar analogy to hang on this thing? he thought with disgust. Jeez, no wonder Claire had left him.

And that's when it hit Nick—finally—why she had turned down his proposal all those years ago. It wasn't because she hadn't loved him. It wasn't because she hadn't wanted to spend the rest of her life with him. It was because she'd known back then that with her intelligence and her ambition and her drive, she could someday give herself a life like this. A life surrounded by luxurious, expensive things, in a huge, expensive house. A life of respect and recognition. Of wealth and affluence. Of beauty and ease. A life she could be proud of.

The kind of life Nick Campisano would never, ever, be able to give her himself.

"That's it, isn't it?" he said softly, unable to mask his surprise at the discovery, voicing his thoughts out loud.

She narrowed her eyes at him in confusion. "What's it? What are you talking about?"

He expelled an errant, incredulous sound as he shook his head slowly back and forth. "I finally get it, Claire."

But her confusion only compounded. "Finally get what?" she asked.

He hesitated only a moment before charging, ''I finally understand what it was you tried to tell me twelve years ago. Why you wouldn't marry me then.''

''You do?'' she asked, her uncertainty still very clear. ''Um, forgive me if I find your comprehension a little surprising. It has, after all, sort of come out of nowhere.''

''Not really,'' he said. ''It's been there right in front of me for twelve years, but I'm just now beginning to see it.''

''You've lost me completely,'' she said. ''See what?''

''You couldn't handle the simple life, could you?'' he told her plainly. ''You wanted more. You wanted money, and recognition and respect. You wanted to be Dr. Claire Wainwright, physician to the rich and famous. Not Mrs. Dominic Campisano, wife and mother of six in Gloucester City, New Jersey. That's why you left me, isn't it, Claire? Because you wanted upward mobility instead of the status quo.''

Claire eyed Nick with complete incredulity, unable to believe he could think such a thing. *This* was the conclusion he'd drawn about their relationship? *This* was what he'd decided had motivated her? *This* was the kind of person he thought her to be? That she was so shallow and superficial, she'd choose a life of luxury and wealth and ease over the kind of lifestyle he'd wanted for them?

As if her life were in any way luxurious, she thought morosely. As if her life were in any way wealthy. In any way easy. Yes, she might have a nice house and a lot of money, but how stupid could he be to think that those were what she valued most in the world?

And how narrow-minded could he be to think she would surrender her own identity in order to assume his? Even if she'd married him, Claire would have aspired to be something other than Mrs. Dominic Campisano. For God's sake.

In addition to everything else he'd wanted her to sacrifice, he would have had her giving up her own name.

"Don't be an idiot, Nick."

His eyebrows shot up in surprise at her charge. "I'm being an idiot?" he asked, his outrage growing. "*I'm* being an idiot?"

She nodded. "Yeah, you're being an idiot. For one thing, how could you think I'd choose money over you?"

"Because that's exactly what you did."

She shook her head. "No, I didn't."

He expelled another incredulous, disappointed sound. "Of course you did. Just look around you."

"Hey, maybe I've taken advantage of my financial situation," she agreed readily, "but I didn't make my decision about us twelve years ago just because I set out to be rich."

"Didn't you?"

"Of course not. And secondly," she rushed on, before he had a chance to contradict her again, "how could you think I'd become Mrs. Dominic Campisano once we got married? *If* we got married," she hastened to clarify.

His outrage disappeared, to be replaced by total confusion. "Well, who the hell else would you be?" he demanded.

This time Claire was the one to mutter a sound of disbelief. "Gee, just a shot in the dark here, Nick, but, um…maybe I'd be Claire Wainwright."

His eyebrows shot up again, nearly disappearing into his hairline. "You'd have actually kept your maiden name after we got married?"

Boy, that just went to show how little attention he'd paid to her all those years ago, Claire thought. She sighed, letting go of some of her pent-up tension with the long, slow breath of air. "Um, Nick?" she asked.

"Yeah, Claire?"

"This may come as a real surprise to you, but, um, not too many people refer to a single woman's name as her 'maiden name' anymore."

That, too, seemed to throw him for a loop, because his mouth dropped open in clear astonishment at hearing such an earth-shattering revelation. "They don't?"

Claire shook her head.

"Then…what do they call it?"

"Oh, they pretty much just refer to a single woman's last name as her 'last name' now. The same way they do single men. Revolutionary, I know, but… There you have it just the same."

"Oh."

"And you know, *my* name, even back then, was a really good name," she added. "It was *my* name. It's still *my* name. The one my parents—the people who gave me life— bestowed upon me when I was born. Why should I change it, just because I get married? And the way you would have had it, I would have lost both my last *and* first names."

Poor Nick. His head was obviously reeling from all these befuddling, newfangled discoveries. "Well," he said, "maybe because…um, because…because that's what women do…when they…get…married?"

Strangely, his total uncertainty and confusion comforted Claire in a way nothing else that evening had. Poor Nick, she thought again. A forties kind of guy, born a couple of decades too late. She supposed she should take pity on him. Go easy on him. Thing was, though, there were a lot of people out there who *hadn't* missed the women's movement. A lot of people who *had* been conscious for and paying attention to the last three decades. Who *did* view the female gender as an equal and formidable force.

But not Nick Campisano. Never Nick Campisano. As

much as she'd loved him, he'd always been a few steps—
or light-years—behind the rest of the world when it came
to women. Of course, if she were honest, she'd admit that
that was probably one of the things she'd loved about him
back then. That he'd been so old-fashioned in that respect.
Unlike so many of the guys she'd known in high school,
Nick had been much more interested in chivalry than he'd
been in Chevrolets. And really, that had been kind of endearing on a teenage guy. On an adult man, however…

Oh, who was she kidding? It was still kind of endearing,
Claire thought. Unrealistic, but endearing. And just like
that, her fury evaporated.

Unfortunately, her certainty that she made the right decision twelve years ago, that the two of them would never
work out together, returned full force. Not because Nick
was blue-collar, the way he seemed to think. Not because
he couldn't give her what he thought she wanted from life.
She didn't want what he thought she did. She hadn't set
out to garner wealth. She hadn't set out to buy a big house
and expensive furniture. She hadn't set out to gain an up-
per-class lifestyle. Those were all simply incidental to the
line of work she had chosen. Had she excelled at something
else, or been interested in some other line of work, she
would have been satisfied with whatever that career had
afforded her.

Okay, so maybe Nick was half-right. Although she
wasn't necessarily interested in riches, she did indeed, very
much, crave respect and recognition. Even there, however,
he wasn't quite correct in his thinking. Because it wasn't
that she wanted respect and recognition from other people
for the job she performed or the way she lived. She wanted
respect and recognition from Nick—for being the individual that she was. Whoever, whatever, that individual might
choose to be.

"Forget about it, Nick," she heard herself say softly. Though she couldn't remember exactly when she'd chosen to speak, or what she'd decided to say. Still, the admonition was worthwhile. There was no point in pursuing what they'd once had. Even if they couldn't quite leave it in the past, either.

"It's not going to happen between us," she added, her voice sounding sad, even to her own ears. "What you and I once had together, maybe we can't completely end it. But we can't just take up where we left off, either. And we can't quite bridge the chasm that the last twelve years has opened up between us. Because the crack that created that chasm has been there since the beginning, Nick, whether either of us wants to admit that or not."

He studied her in silence for a long time, his hands settled loosely on his hips, his lips turned down in consternation, his eyes blazing with…what? She wasn't quite sure she should even try to identify it.

"You don't think we could build a bridge?" he finally asked, his voice belying nothing of what he might be feeling or thinking.

Slowly, silently, she shook her head.

"You don't think there's any point in even trying?"

Again she shook her head. "Don't tell me you do."

"Don't I?" he asked.

His response surprised her. And when he said nothing further to clarify his meaning, the flutter of something distant and dangerous rippled through her soul. For one brief, odd moment, the entire world seemed to slip away—all time, all matter, everything. There was only Claire and Nick, and the feelings each generated. Old feelings, new feelings, feelings that were a blend of each. And in that brief, odd moment, she felt as if she were twenty-two years old again, and that maybe, just maybe…

''*Do* you?'' she asked further, before she could stop herself, her voice so soft and so full of hope, she could scarcely identify it as her own.

For a long moment he didn't alter his pose at all, didn't move, didn't react, didn't speak. The only movement from him Claire detected was the rapid rise and fall of his chest, as if he were struggling to breathe deeply and evenly. His dark eyes were cold and flat, his mouth—that sexy, incredible mouth—was in no way inviting. He seemed to be a million miles away.

Then suddenly he jerked himself out of whatever reverie he'd descended into and crossed the spare room in a quick, half-dozen strides. He didn't even look at Claire as he pushed past her into the hallway, didn't say a word about where he was going or what he planned to do. Before she realized what was happening, he had disappeared around the corner, and she could hear the rapid, steady, *thump-thump-thump* of his footfalls on the stairs.

And only then, when she stood completely alone in the spare bedroom of her big, luxurious, beautiful—silent and lonely—house, did she realize he'd never really answered her question at all.

Five

When Claire opened her eyes the following morning, she wasn't sure at first what had awoken her or why she felt so tired and disoriented when she did awaken. For a moment, she only lay in her bed, still half-asleep, and gazed at the faint sunlight that filtered through the filmy ivory sheers on her window. She wondered what time it was and why it felt so late. Gradually it dawned on her that she'd had a very strange and wondrous dream as she'd slept. One filled with snow and holidays, and fuzzy odds and ends, and then…Nick Campisano. How odd. It had been months since she'd dreamed about Nick.

Then a sound unlike anything she'd ever heard before met her ears, rousing her a bit more. No, wait, she thought, still feeling a little muzzy-headed. She *had* heard that sound before. And not too long ago, if memory served. It was a soft sound. A warm sound. A quiet sound. A…a baby sound.

Oh, no. No, no, no, no, no…

Immediately Claire snapped to complete consciousness. And immediately the panic that had been too close a companion the night before began to rise to greet her again. Reluctantly she rolled her body over on the mattress, ready to scoot to the other side and peek down into the basket she recalled placing on the floor there some hours ago.

But the moment she completed the action, she realized she wasn't alone in her room. Not just because there was a baby present, but because Nick sat in the rocking chair, as he had the night before—or rather, the way he had earlier that morning—cradling said baby in his arms.

She was dressed in one of her little pink outfits, and had the chubby little fingers of one hand curled loosely around the wrist that held the bottle from which she was hungrily sucking. With her other hand, she was reaching out toward Nick's face, and he, in turn, was smiling down at her. With her shock of dark hair—sticking straight up like Don King's, Claire noted with a reluctant grin—the baby might well have been his own daughter. And with those big blue eyes, she might well have been Claire's daughter, too.

"Good morning," Nick said without looking up at her.

Oh, no. Nick was in her bedroom. Had been in her bedroom for some time now, judging from the looks of it. Had been there while she was sleeping. Had he *watched* her while she was sleeping? she wondered frantically. Had she talked in her sleep while she was dreaming about him? It had been a pretty hot dream in parts, just as all of her dreams about Nick were. Had she said something incriminating? Oh, God, had she drooled?

Hastily Claire glanced down at herself, and was instantly relieved to discover that she was only marginally rumpled from sleep—and that there didn't seem to be anything resembling drool stains on her pajama top or pillowcase. At least, she was only marginally rumpled from the neck down, she thought further. Heaven knew what she looked like from the neck *up*. Hopefully she didn't have a bad case of bed hair, as she usually did in the morning. And hopefully her face wasn't creased from the wrinkles in her pillowcase. And hopefully she didn't look as exhausted and beleaguered as she felt.

Oh, who was she kidding? she thought morosely. She probably looked *worse* than she felt. She couldn't remember the last time she'd awoken feeling rested and relaxed and at peace. And what did she care what she looked like, anyway? she berated herself further. She didn't need to look nice for Nick. She didn't need to look rested and relaxed and at peace for him.

That's right. That irritating little voice popped up again. *Because, hey, Nick has seen the way you look when you wake up lots of times, hasn't he? He's already seen you at your worst. And, even at that, he* still *loved you. Go figure.*

Or at least he had *said* he loved her, she reminded the voice grumpily. And a guy his age back then, with hormones raging, who was getting sex from a girl on a regular basis? A guy like that would have said anything to keep the girl in question happy.

Immediately Claire felt guilty for the uncharitable thought. Nick hadn't been like that at all. He had genuinely loved her back then. She was just feeling cranky and annoyed because a few hours of sleep hadn't been nearly enough to make her feel human, yet there sat Nick, bathed in sunlight, looking gorgeous and rested and yummy.

He had changed his clothes from the evening—or rather, morning—before, and she wondered where the tattered, faded green sweatshirt that now topped his blue jeans had come from.

"I had some gym clothes in the Jeep," he said, as if

reading her mind. "Clean ones," he hastened to add. "I always keep a spare change with me, because I usually stop at the gym a few times a week to work out, on my the way home. Last night, with the snow and all, I didn't make it."

The *and all,* of course, would have been the call Claire had made to report the abandoned baby. She nodded her understanding, then lifted a hand to smooth her fingers over…uh-oh…over what felt like some extremely bumpy bed hair.

"Um," she began eloquently. She swiped a hand through her bangs and tried again. "Uh, good morning."

"Sleep well?" Nick asked, still focusing on the baby instead of Claire.

"Not really," she replied honestly.

"Did you at least have sweet dreams?"

She eyed him suspiciously, wondering if he really was reading her thoughts, or if she really had talked in her sleep. He'd always had a knack for knowing what she was thinking, she recalled now, too late. "Um, no," she lied. "I didn't dream at all."

"I did."

She decided not to pursue that, and instead asked, "How's our little tax deduction doing this morning?"

"She's fine," Nick said with a chuckle. And with that, he finally did glance up at Claire. Immediately, however, his smile fell and his expression changed from one of affectionate warmth to one of heated recognition. "She's fine," he repeated, his voice dropping both in pitch and in volume. "And so are you."

Claire emitted an anxious, doubtful sound. "Oh, right," she muttered. "Nick, I've seen myself first thing in the morning. I know better than to believe that I'm fine."

"I've seen you in the morning, too, Claire," he rallied quickly. "Lots of times if you'll recall."

"More than a decade ago," she hastened to add.

"Yeah, and you look even better now than you did then."

"Oh, right," she repeated. But she couldn't quite stop the warm fizzle of heat that wandered through her entire body at his words, at his look. Gee, waking up every morning to have a man like that give you a look like that... Well, it was certainly something a woman could get used to, Claire thought.

Of course, *she* shouldn't get used to it. She couldn't get used to it. She *wouldn't* get used to it. Because there was no point in thinking that she and Nick might be able to salvage anything of what they'd had when they were kids. He was just passing through her life right now, she reminded herself. Just as he had passed through it a handful of other times since they'd split up. He hadn't changed from his old ways at all, and really, neither had she. He still didn't take her seriously as an independent woman, and she still insisted on being taken seriously that way. He still didn't understand who she was deep down, and she craved that understanding from him.

More to the point, it was obvious that he still wanted things that she didn't want herself—lots of kids, a stay-at-home wife, a life like his parents had had. And Claire... Well, even if she couldn't quite put her finger on exactly *what* she wanted, she knew it wasn't that.

"How long have you been up?" she asked him.

He shrugged and returned his attention to the baby, who was swallowing the last of the formula. "Not long. About fifteen or twenty minutes. I heard Sleeping Beauty here wake up, and when I didn't hear you waking up with her, I realized you were even more exhausted than I was. So I got up and got dressed and came in here to feed the little princess."

He got dressed, Claire reflected, homing in on that part of his statement more than any other. Which meant that he hadn't been dressed when he woke. Which meant that he'd been…*un*dressed. Which meant that he'd been…naked. In her spare bed. Between her spare sheets. Those sheets that she sometimes put on her own bed. Oh, dear…

"Thanks," Claire said, hoping her voice didn't really sound as strangled as she thought it did. "For getting up with the baby, I mean," she hurried to clarify, just in case he really was reading her thoughts this morning, and had picked up on that naked-between-her-sheets business. "I, uh…" She cleared her throat indelicately. "I appreciate it. I can't believe I didn't hear her waking up."

It was yet another indication that she was lousy mother material, she thought further to herself. She didn't even wake up when a baby was calling out her need to be fed. Oh, yeah. Great maternal instincts at work there. She was right up there with Ma Barker and Medea.

Nick hefted the baby up onto his shoulder. "Actually, I'm not surprised you slept through it. She wasn't making much noise," he told her. "It's funny, how she doesn't seem to cry much. Any other baby, left with strangers, would probably be throwing one fit after another. But this one doesn't seem to be too bothered by us at all."

"Maybe she's just genetically gregarious," Claire offered.

"Or maybe she just senses she has nothing to fear here."

"Well, nothing now that you're here," Claire pointed out. "Before your arrival, she was anything but relaxed and comforted. She *was* throwing a fit when all she had to rely on was me."

Yep, lousy mothering instincts, Claire thought. Even a little baby could pick up on that right away. No point dwelling on it, though. It wasn't as if it was something she didn't already know about herself. She ought to be grateful Nick had shown up when he did. In fact, she *was* grateful Nick had shown up. But only because of the baby, of course, she hastily qualified. No other reason than that.

"She probably just sensed your panic last night," Nick said, graciously giving Claire a way out.

But Claire knew better. "Smart baby," she said. "Because I *was* panicked last night."

"That's only natural, under the circumstances," he told her. "Now that you're more relaxed, so is the baby."

"Who says I'm relaxed?"

"Aren't you?"

Claire chuckled anxiously. "Oh, come on, Nick. I haven't been relaxed in twelve years."

He eyed her thoughtfully. "Interesting timing."

She eyed him back, with irritation. "I meant since I started med school."

"Sure you did."

"I *did*."

He adopted an expression of total innocence. "Okay, fine, Claire. Whatever you say."

She was spared having to say anything more, because the baby chose that moment to let loose with a rousing burp of almost meteorological proportions, something that made all three of them laugh. The baby pushed away from Nick's shoulder and smiled hugely, a gesture that made something go all soft and gooey inside Claire.

"She really is adorable, isn't she?" she said, unable—and unwilling—to hide the smile that came with the realization.

The baby tweaked Nick's nose again, then laughed harder. "Yeah, she's a pistol, all right," he concurred.

"I wonder what her name is? It's strange that there was nothing in her belongings to tell us anything about—"

"Haley," Nick interrupted.

Claire arched her eyebrows in surprise. "How do you know her name is Haley? Did she tell you that? I mean, I know I don't know much about babies, but even *I* was under the impression that that talking business didn't start quite this early."

Before Nick could answer her, the baby started bouncing up and down in his lap like a jack-in-the-box. He held her while she moved, but gave her free rein to jump to her heart's delight. And her expression was clearly delighted, indicating that this activity was something new and exciting that she had only recently discovered, and now she couldn't wait to share it with the rest of the world. As she jumped up and down, Nick laughed, and on one particularly spectacular leap, he turned her to face Claire. And that was when she saw that the little romper the baby was wearing had the word *Haley* embroidered over the left pocket.

"Oh," she said.

"And speaking of which," Nick told her pointedly, "in addition to changing her clothes, this is the second time in a row that I changed her diaper. You owe me two now, radioactive or not."

"Fine," Claire conceded, knowing full well that she had plenty of time between now and then to fabricate an excuse for why she would do no such thing. At least, she was pretty sure she had plenty of time. Just how often did babies—

"A couple of the other sleepers and stuff have this kind of hand-done decoration on them, too," Nick added, interrupting her thoughts. "Looks like her mama or somebody has a real talent for this kind of thing."

"Looks like her mama—or somebody—took a lot of care in doing that," Claire added meaningfully. "A lot of *loving* care."

Nick frowned. "Yeah, well, like I said. Somebody did. Maybe a grandmother."

"Why don't you think it was her mother?"

He shrugged. "Seems kind of contradictory, doesn't it? Spend a lot of time and loving care embroidering your kid's stuff, then abandon her with those things in the worst snowfall in Jersey history."

"I told you the mother didn't leave until she was sure the baby would be taken inside," Claire reminded him carefully.

Nick met her gaze levelly. "She still left, though, didn't she?"

Claire sighed heavily. "Yes. Yes, she did. But who knows what her situation was, Nick? I just don't think we should come down too hard on her until we know all the facts. There may have been extenuating circumstances that drove the mother to this. I doubt very seriously this was something she just decided to do on a whim."

He focused his attention on the baby again. "I don't care what the mother's circumstances were. What kind of person could look at a sweet little thing like this and dump her? Just answer me that."

Halfheartedly, Claire offered, "I don't know. A scared kid. Somebody who honestly thought abandoning the baby would be the best thing for her. Maybe the mother was sick," she proposed. "Maybe she didn't have a home. Maybe the baby's father drove her to it. Maybe he was mistreating them both. Maybe she thought this was a loving gesture—protecting her child, getting her daughter the kind of life she couldn't give the baby herself.

"I don't know," she said again, spreading her arms wide in defeat and frustration. "I just feel like this wasn't a malicious act. It was a desperate attempt on the mother's part to help her baby when she couldn't offer that help herself.

If it had been malicious,'' she added soberly, ''the baby would have been found elsewhere. And probably not in very good shape.''

''Yeah, well, we'll get it all settled when we find the mother,'' Nick said, sitting the baby on his lap again so that Haley faced Claire.

''Do you really think you'll find her?''

He met her gaze levelly. ''To be honest, I doubt it. It's hard to trace this kind of thing. Haley's not a newborn, so there's not much potential to check hospitals for recent births. We can only hope that someone who knows the mother gets suspicious over why that mother suddenly doesn't have a baby anymore, and then calls the authorities.''

''Do you think that's going to happen?''

''I don't know,'' he told her. ''If the mother's a runaway, I doubt we'll have much luck. The best thing that could happen—for us *and* the mother—is for the mother to turn herself in.''

''What happens then?''

''Depends.''

''On what?''

''On the situation. If she seems like she's genuinely sorry she abandoned the baby, and if it seems like she really has the potential to be a good parent, a judge might see fit to enroll her in a program that would help her learn to take care of her child.''

''That would be good,'' Claire said, heartening some.

''Or she might lose the baby,'' Nick qualified. ''Another judge might disregard any plea on the mother's part, find her unfit and put the baby into foster care.''

''That would be bad.''

''Maybe. Maybe not.''

"You don't sound as convinced of the mother's villainy as you did a little while ago."

He shrugged again, watching the baby as she leaned forward, reached for the laces of his hiking boot, and tried to stuff them into her mouth. Gently Nick pulled her back into a standing position. "You could be right about there being extenuating circumstances," he said. "I didn't think about the baby's father. Maybe he was dangerous. Or maybe the mother is homeless. Maybe she's sick. I'll reserve judgment for now."

Wow, Claire thought. Nick had stopped just short of saying that he might have been *wrong*. She'd never in her life seen him do such a thing. When they were kids, it really had been Nick's way or no way. He'd never once conceded to any potential for being wrong. To Nick's way of thinking, he *wasn't* wrong. Not ever. Of course, for the most part Claire had always agreed with him on most things. Not their future, but on other things.

Still, he'd obviously come a long way in his thinking if he could admit that he may have jumped the gun on something. That in itself was a major milestone for him.

Claire turned her attention back to the baby. She really was a sweetheart. And she seemed to be such a happy, contented, outgoing little thing, another indication that her mother probably wasn't the soulless, selfish creature that Nick had initially wanted to make her out to be.

"Still, it's odd that Haley's mother would have left her here without a note of explanation," Claire said, speaking her thoughts aloud. "But I sorted through everything, half hoping there might be a letter or *something* describing the situation." She shrugged. "There was nothing. Just the basic life-sustaining necessities."

"Could there be something else outside?" he asked.

"I didn't think to look," she admitted. "With all the

snow and everything, I just brought the basket and baby inside without giving it another thought.''

"I didn't see anything when I went out to the Jeep this morning,'' Nick added. "Then again, I wasn't looking for anything. Now that it's daylight, it might not be a bad idea to go outside and have a look around.''

Claire turned her attention to the window. "Is it still snowing?''

Nick nodded. "Yeah, like a big dog.''

"Great.''

"I could still give it a shot. Wouldn't hurt to look. You could feed Sleeping Beauty here something a little more substantial while I do my job and investigate the premises.''

The easy feeling of well-being that had begun to seep into Claire evaporated immediately at his suggestion. "Me?'' she said. "Feed that baby? As in real baby food? From real baby food jars?''

He rolled his eyes. "No, I meant fake baby food from invisible baby food jars. Some of that virtual baby food you can just pluck off the Internet these days. That kind of baby food.''

Claire narrowed her eyes at him suspiciously. "They make virtual baby food now and sell it on the Internet?''

Nick gaped at her for a moment, then started to laugh outright, a rumble of warm humor that seemed to bubble up from his very soul. And although Haley couldn't possibly have gotten the joke, she smiled, too, punctuating Nick's merriment with a few little baby chuckles of her own.

It was, Claire decided, really, really cute.

"Boy, you really *don't* know anything about babies, do you?'' he asked through his laughter.

She expelled an impatient sound. "Didn't I say that? Like twenty times? You still don't listen, do you, Nick?"

"I listen just fine, thanks," he assured her, quickly sobering. "As usual, though, you just don't make any sense."

Claire gritted her teeth at him. *"Don't start, Nick."*

He held up one hand, palm out, in a gesture of surrender. But all he said was, "You can do this, Claire. You can feed the baby."

"I don't know...."

Nick laughed at what she knew must be her terrified expression. She knew that was what her expression was, because what she was feeling at the moment was, well... terrified.

"Oh, come on," he cajoled. "What's the big deal?"

"I...I...I don't know how to feed a baby. I don't even know how to do the bottle thing. There's no way I could manage the solid food thing."

"It's as easy as opening a jar, plopping some gooky stuff out into a bowl, dipping a spoon into it and putting spoon— with food—into the baby's mouth."

She eyed him warily. "You make it sound easy."

"That's because it *is* easy, Claire."

She studied him intently for a moment. "I don't trust you."

He gazed at her with what was clearly feigned innocence. "Why not?"

"Because."

"Because why?"

"Because you always say things are easy when they're not, that's why."

"Oh, come on, Claire. She's just a baby. A teensy-weensy, little-bitty, ookum-snookum baby."

She frowned at him. "And you're talking like a moron. That's a dead giveaway, Nick."

He eyed her pointedly. "You can do this," he said again. "It'll be a piece of cake. Or a bowl of rice cereal. Whatever."

Claire inhaled deeply and released the breath in a long, thoughtful sigh, her gaze never veering from Nick's face. He was hiding something. She could tell that much. But he was right. Haley was just a little baby. There was no reason to be afraid. All Claire had to do was shovel a few spoonfuls of rice cereal—and maybe some applesauce or something—into the adorable sweetheart's little mouth.

That didn't sound so hard, she thought. Really, what could possibly go wrong?

Those words came back to haunt Claire—in a big way—a couple of hours later. It was while she was trying—without much success—to scrape petrified rice cereal off of her kitchen ceiling. And off of her kitchen floor. And her kitchen table. Her kitchen countertops. Kitchen cabinets. Appliances. Paddle fan. Light fixture. Windows. And the Mary Englebreit calendar that said "It's Good to Be a Queen."

And while she was performing this Herculean and fruitless deed, there sat Nick, all nice and clean and perky—damn him—a laughing baby Haley in his lap, looking the very picture of domestic bliss.

"Honestly, Nick, you might have warned me," Claire said as she scrubbed at a particularly nasty spot of the alleged baby food that had fused—evidently forever—with her microwave. "If the Pentagon only knew what kind of weapon this stuff could be...."

Nick chuckled. "C'mon, Claire, it's only baby food," he said. "Rice cereal. It's nutritious. Says so, right on the box."

"Nutritious like a cinder block maybe," she muttered. "I could weatherize my garage with this stuff."

He laughed again. "Well, she seemed to like the applesauce."

"Yeah, what little didn't land in my lap," Claire agreed, eyeing the huge, round stain made up of two semicircles, on her pajama top and pajama bottoms. She ran a restless hand through her—very sticky—hair. "And what little didn't land on my head," she added derisively. "I think I need a shower."

"Good idea," Nick said. "I know that one I had did me a world of good."

Yeah, she just bet it did. Nick had come in from his pointless search of the front yard, looking fit and alert and full of life, with snow clinging to his dark hair, his cheeks ruddy from the cold, his breathing ebullient from his physical exertion. Yep, he'd come in, had taken one look at the scene playing out in the kitchen—the scene that had called for mass quantities of applesauce and that mysterious epoxy known as rice cereal, flying about in all directions—and had said something along the lines of "Whoa, Claire. Looks like you've got everything under control here, so I'll just hit the showers," and promptly disappeared.

Oh, sure. Prime candidate for fatherhood he was, all right.

"Yes, well," she said, valiantly reining in the multitude of commentary she wanted to offer, "I think I'll do just that. Shower, I mean. Shampoo. Soap up. Shave. Scrape. Squeegee. Whatever it takes to get this stuff off of me."

Again Nick laughed and, just like that, any irritation Claire was feeling completely evaporated. He had the most wonderful laugh. Deep, easy, uninhibited, frequent. The fact that he'd never been one to hide his feelings—good or bad—had always been something about him that she'd envied. She'd never been comfortable with excessive emotions herself, even good ones. Even things like love and happiness. Too much emotion could be terrifying. Too much emotion made a person lose control, and Claire didn't like surrendering control. Not to anybody.

In spite of that, there had been many times when she'd lost control around Nick. Not just sexually, although that had certainly happened often enough, but emotionally, too. He'd made her feel deeply and uninhibitedly about many things. Mostly about Nick, of course, but also about life. There had been times when she had indeed been terrified of how easy it had been to let go with him. Terrified, because she just didn't understand those feelings at all.

She still wasn't sure she understood. She loved her parents, and she knew they loved her. But it had never been the Wainwright custom to be overly emotional about anything. Wainwrights simply didn't show how they felt. It was no big deal. It just wasn't how they did things. Campisanos, on the other hand, wore their emotions on their sleeves—in big, neon, capital letters—for all the world to see.

Neither way was necessarily right or wrong, she knew. But they *were* very, very different. And it wasn't easy for one type of person to fall in love with the other type. Nor was it easy to unlearn old ways, or to give up and leave behind what had always been a way of life.

Really, neither of them *should* have to change in order to be happy, she thought. She and Nick should be able to get along just fine the way they were. Then again, it hadn't been their different ways of expressing themselves that had split them up, had it? It had been the fact that they envisioned entirely different futures together. They'd wanted entirely different things.

Claire was getting a headache, which was actually nothing new. Her high-stress job and solitary way of life were both conducive to physical ailments like headaches. Backaches. Chest pains. The usual. She knew that both as a physician, and as a human being. Living the way she did wasn't really living at all. Oh, sure, the job was gratifying and fulfilling and meaningful. And yes, she had a lovely home and money in the bank and a financial plan for the future.

But really, what good was all that when she had no one with whom to share any of it? And how was she supposed to deal with the physical pain—never mind the emotional pain, which was just as bad—when she had no release for the tension and pent-up anxiety?

"You okay?"

Nick's question, so deceptive in its simplicity, made Claire want to laugh. No, on second thought, it made her want to cry. Because she realized then that no, she wasn't okay. That it had been a long, long time since she had been okay. And she had no idea what to do to make herself feel better.

"You look kind of ragged," he clarified further. "You want to go back to bed? Try to get a little more sleep? I can handle this crowd."

"No, I'm fine," she lied, dropping her hand back down to her side. "But I think I will take a shower and get dressed."

She glanced up at the clock. It was just past eleven. It had been snowing now for more than twenty-four hours straight. That thought drove her gaze to the window, where she saw no indication that the fat wet flakes would be lessening anytime soon.

"What do you think the chances are that someone will be able to come and get that baby today?" she asked, dreading the answer she knew was coming.

Nick hesitated a moment before saying, "Not good, I'm afraid. But I'll try making a few more phone calls while you're in the shower."

She nodded, hoping for the best, preparing for the worst. Funny thing was, though, suddenly she couldn't quite distinguish best from worst. She wasn't sure which was which or what was what. She had no idea how she felt about anything.

Fatigue, she told herself. When people got this exhausted, they had no idea what they felt. Their thoughts were jumbled, and their sense of right and wrong was completely blurred. She shouldn't even be trying to gauge her feelings right now. She was sure to wind up more confused than ever.

"I'll be in the shower," she said softly, moving slowly toward the kitchen door. "Just…just see what you can do while I'm in there."

Six

What Nick wanted to do while Claire was in the shower, Claire didn't want to know, he thought as he watched her leave the kitchen. Because what he wanted to do right then was tuck the baby into her basket for a nice, *loooong* snooze, follow Claire up the stairs and into the bathroom, into the shower, under the hot spray of water, with no clothes to be had on either of them, and take his time soaping every inch of her sweet—

And *boy,* those weren't thoughts any man should be having in the presence of a minor.

He glanced down at baby Haley and smiled. "What are we gonna do with you?" he said softly.

In response, she circled her lips into a perfect O and said, "Ooooooooo."

Nick nodded. "Yeah, that's what I was thinking, too. How about we tour the castle grounds while Queen Claire is in the shower? I don't think she'll mind, and it'll keep you occupied for a bit, and then I can make my phone calls.'' He dipped his head and pressed his forehead lightly to Haley's. She, in turn, grabbed a fistful of his hair and tugged playfully. ''At six or seven months,'' he added conspiratorially, ''entertainment for you is *not* that hard to find.''

After gently rubbing noses with her, he hefted the baby against his shoulder and stood, but Haley squiggled and wriggled around until she was cradled in his arm the opposite way, gazing out in front of her instead of behind, over Nick's shoulder.

''Oh, so you want to see where you're going instead of where you've been, huh?'' he asked with a chuckle. ''That's a good sign.''

In response, Haley gurgled a few incoherent syllables and drooled on her romper. Nick laughed harder. He couldn't get over how sweet-natured this kid was. Any other baby, abandoned and taken in by strangers, would probably be howling and timid and fearful. But not Haley. No way. She was one tough Jersey girl.

And one big cutie, too. He wondered if there was any way to tame that shock of dark hair sticking straight up like a bonfire on top of her head, then decided that he didn't even want to try. Somehow, the funky do just added to her personality. Like her big blue eyes and huge, toothless grin.

Too bad her future was so uncertain, he thought, sobering. A baby like this deserved better.

Nick decided to put that troubling thought out of his mind for now and focus on the present instead. He had promised Haley a tour, and, by golly, he was going to give her one. Never mind that he had no idea where he was going. Never mind that this wasn't even his place to be showing off. He and Claire went *waaaaaay* back, he reasoned. She wouldn't mind if he and the baby explored a little.

"Okay, so here we have the kitchen," he said, sweeping his arm out magnanimously. "You couldn't possibly know this," he added parenthetically, "seeing as how you have such a limited life experience, but I happen to know for a fact that this particular kitchen is larger than most suburban living rooms."

"Oooooo," Haley said.

Nick nodded. "My sentiments, exactly."

The baby also couldn't know that this room was probably more expensively decorated than most suburban living rooms, too, what with all the state-of-the-art appliances and terra-cotta flooring, and tiled countertops and mosaic backsplash, and wallpaper with a pattern reminiscent of a Greek Island getaway.

Man, Claire had spared no expense when decorating this place. It was definitely a dream house, created and designed with tender loving care. It was the kind of house a person created because they wanted to stay here forever, surrounded by family, marking all those milestones that came with living life. It was the kind of place to fill with happy memories of raising a family, then sit back and enjoy those memories when all the kids were grown and gone. It was the kind of house that would be perfect for welcoming grandchildren.

Best not to think about that stuff, Nick thought, cutting himself off as a ribbon of melancholy unrolled inside him. Claire had made it clear that she wanted no part of that big family free-for-all business, so there was no point in seeing things that just weren't there. Claire had made her home the way it was, because that was the way *she* wanted it. Period. There was no sense creating a fantasy that would never materialize.

"Okay, so out here," Nick continued, walking with the baby into the hallway, "we have what's known as a hallway."

"Oooooo," Haley commented.

"Yeah, as hallways go, this is a pretty nice one," he concurred, noting for the first time, in more than passing, anyway, the intricate parquetry and the array of snapshots scattered across both slate blue walls.

He hadn't planned on studying the photo gallery for any length of time, but his gaze lit on one picture that made him stop dead in his tracks. It was a snapshot of him and Claire and his two brothers, sitting on the back stoop of the Campisano home in Deptford. Nick was smiling devilishly as he held up his hand behind her head with two fingers extended, and she was laughing as she reached behind herself to stop him. His brothers, too, were laughing uproariously. Their mother had taken the photo the summer after Claire's graduation from high school, and they had all been enormously happy.

And enormously oblivious, he thought with a sad smile. Still, it was a great shot, one that perfectly captured the rapture of youth. Too bad people had to grow up, he thought. Too bad, things had to change.

But he and Claire *had* grown up, he mused. And things had definitely changed. Then again, there was a lot to be said for the here and now, even with the uncertainty and differences of opinion that still simmered between them. Maybe, just maybe, change wasn't such a bad thing after all.

A brief inspection of the other photos revealed numerous friends and relations of Claire's whom Nick didn't recognize, and a handful whom he did, and two more pictures that set his heart to humming wildly. One was of him and Claire both taken at Ocean City shortly after they'd started dating. And one was of him alone, seated beneath a tree, the late-afternoon sun bathing his face with pinks and yellows and oranges, lighting bright fires in the highlights of his hair.

It was an intimate photo, one that revealed quite clearly how much he loved her. Because Claire had been the one who was taking the picture that day, and Nick hadn't bothered to hide how he was feeling.

The realization that she hadn't completely erased him from her life, that she had in fact framed a photo like this, and had hung it in a place she passed every day on her way to the kitchen—even if it was only one of scores of photos of her life—went a long way toward making him feel better about things. Maybe there was still a chance to mend the rift between them, he thought. Maybe there was still a chance the two of them could work things out.

Maybe there was still a chance that Claire loved him as much as he loved her.

Because it hit Nick then—not too surprisingly, really— that he was most definitely still in love with Claire. That the feelings he'd had for her when they were teenagers hadn't faded one whit. On the contrary, as he'd grown and matured over the years, so had his love for her. That was why he'd never married, why he'd never even come close. Because he'd never felt for another woman what he had felt for Claire so many years ago. What he continued to feel for Claire to this day.

And now maybe, just maybe, fate had thrown him a curve that he could play. Maybe, just maybe, he had a chance to put things to rights between them. Provided, of course, Claire wanted that, too.

A none-too-gentle tug on his hair reminded him that, for now, he had another female he needed to focus his attention on, and he gazed down at Haley with a smile. ''Maybe,'' he said to her, "you could give me a hand here in convincing Claire to give me a second chance. What do you say?"

In response, Haley offered him a dimpled smile that gave him the impression she was with him one hundred percent. Impulsively he dropped a quick kiss on the crown of her head, then the two of them continued on their exploration. They made a quick tour of the living room, since Haley had already seen that part of the house, then crossed the foyer to a small library whose shelves were overflowing with books.

"Sorry, kid," Nick said as he quickly scanned the titles. "No *Pat the Bunny* or *Fox in Socks* to be had." He pulled one cloth-bound tome from a shelf at eye level. *"Fear of Flying,"* he read from the spine. "Nope, don't think you're quite ready for that one yet. So on with the tour," he added as he replaced the book on the shelf.

They made their way through a music room whose centerpiece was a baby grand piano, and Nick remembered that Claire had always wanted to learn to play. Evidently she was fulfilling that dream now, too, he noted, filing away the information with everything else he was learning about her this weekend.

Breezing through the formal dining room—roughly the size of his entire apartment, he couldn't help but realize—they found themselves in a good-size study that Claire seemed to be using as a home office. It was outfitted with a home computer whose screen saver currently scrolled the message, "Call your mother…Call your mother…Call your mother…," and shelves filled with medical texts and models of body parts Nick thought he was probably better off not investigating too closely. Covering the baby's eyes—hey, he didn't care if she *was* female; this stuff was best left for another decade or so—he concluded their tour of the first floor right there.

Upstairs, he bypassed Claire's bedroom, noting that the shower had shut off and the blow dryer was running, then stood in the doorway of, and briefly described for Haley, the room where he had passed the night himself. Beyond that, he discovered two more bedrooms, both of which were as sumptuously decorated as the rest of the house, and neither of which seemed to have been occupied anytime recently.

Nick told himself it was only idle curiosity that made him investigate the closets, and *not* because he needed any reassurance that one of them might contain something like, oh, say…men's clothing, for example. But one of the closets seemed to be stocked with Claire's summer clothes, and the other was filled with what appeared to be boxes of personal files. No men's clothing at all.

Not that *that* was the reason he had checked anyway, natch.

Once again, it struck him how odd it was that Claire had chosen to live in such a huge, cozily decorated house all by herself. Sure, she deserved to reap the benefits of her long education and hard work, and sure she was entitled to surround herself with beautiful things, if she could afford to do so. But the fact that she had done so on such a large, so thoroughly domestic, scale was puzzling, to say the least.

As a single woman who had made it clear she had no desire to procreate, it would have made much more sense for her to buy a smaller place that would be easier to care for, and less spooky at night. Speaking for himself, living alone in a house this size would give Nick a major wiggins. But Claire evidently enjoyed having all this space to herself.

Go figure.

Of course, he couldn't figure, which was what was causing him so much irritation. And somehow he just couldn't shake the feeling that there was a reason for Claire's having made the choices she had, a reason that made perfect sense, if only he could work it all out and—

"Lose something, Nick?"

He was so deeply immersed in thought, so utterly wrapped up in the enigma that was Claire's life, that when he first heard the question, uttered in a feminine voice, he honestly thought Haley had been the one who had offered it. Arrowing his eyebrows downward, he studied the baby's face. Her expression was open and inquisitive, as if she were as interested in his answer as—

"Claire," he said aloud, spinning around to find her gazing at him from the doorway.

Belatedly he realized the closet door was still open, and that his current position probably looked pretty incriminating to the casual observer. Like Claire, for instance.

"What are you doing in here?" she asked.

Her voice held simple curiosity, and nothing more, he noted with some reassurance. Though her posture was a bit on the aggressive side. Her loosely fisted hands were settled on her hips, her legs were spread slightly apart, and her dark brows were arched in a way that was just a trifle menacing.

But that wasn't what Nick noticed most.

What Nick noticed most was that Claire looked unbelievably soft and beautiful, dressed as she was in an oversize, pale blue shirt of some velvety fabric, and a pair of snug, formfitting...whattayacall'em...leggings in the same material. Big ol' socks hugged her feet and were scrunched around her ankles, and she'd pulled her hair back into a high ponytail, bound near the crown of her head with a big wad of fabric.

For one brief instant, she looked exactly the way she had in high school. And in that brief instant, Nick wanted nothing more than to pull her into his arms, hold her close and keep her there forever.

"I, uh..." he began awkwardly. "I mean, Haley and I...we were just...you know..."

"Rifling through my belongings?" Claire supplied helpfully. But there was a small smile dancing about her lips, so he knew she wasn't all *that* angry. At least, he hoped she wasn't.

"No," he assured her hastily. He turned to the baby. "We would never do that, would we, Haley?"

"Noooooo," the baby said, something that drew a suspicious look from Nick.

"What did you say?" he asked.

In response, Haley only stared at him and said nothing whatsoever to clarify her position on the matter.

"You know, you're not supposed to be able to talk yet," he told the infant. "That doesn't come for at least a few more months."

As if this were news to her, Haley opened her eyes wide and stuck three fingers into her mouth, so that she might prevent herself from saying anything more that she wasn't supposed to be able to say.

"I mean it, kid," Nick warned her. "Don't go getting precocious on me."

"That's advice you'd be well-advised to take yourself, Nick," Claire said.

He turned back to face her. "Who, me?"

"Yeah, you."

"You think I'm precocious?"

"You're definitely something."

He smiled rakishly. At least he hoped it was rakishly. It

sure felt rakish. Whatever the hell that was. "Oh, yeah?" he asked.

She nodded. "Oh, yeah."

"Like what? Exactly? Do feel free to go on at length in your description. So long as it's all excessively flattering, I mean."

This time she shook her head. "Not so much precocious," she qualified, "but I think you definitely get ahead of yourself sometimes."

"Can you give me a for instance?"

Instead of answering him, Claire said, "What did you find out from the authorities while I was in the shower?"

Nick groaned and gave his forehead a mental smack. He'd totally forgotten he had promised her he'd do that. "I'm sorry, Claire, I didn't make any calls. Haley and I just started chatting, one thing led to another and then suddenly…" He let his voice trail off.

"And then suddenly you were rifling through my belongings," Claire finished for him.

"No!" he denied quickly. "I wasn't doing that."

She eyed him with much doubt.

"Okay, so we might have checked out a few…you know…"

"Closets?"

"Yeah, well, okay, closets. But it was just idle curiosity, that's all."

"Mmm."

He narrowed his eyes at her. "What's that supposed to mean?"

She shrugged. "Nothing. Just 'Mmm,' that's all."

"Sounded like a lot more than just 'Mmm' to me."

Claire's posture became more threatening. She leaned forward, tightened her fists on her hips and began to tap her foot erratically. "Don't you dare try to put me on the defensive here, Nick. You're the one who's been rifling through my—''

''I was *not* rifling through anything. Claire, you're being—''

Haley began to fret then, obviously responding to the less-than-easygoing mood that had suddenly descended upon the trio. She waved her little hands anxiously in the air and scrunched up her little face and began to make soft sounds of distress.

''Oh, now look what you've done,'' Nick said, bouncing her lightly in an effort to cheer her up. But the action only made her that much more unsettled, and she began to cry in earnest.

''What *I* did?'' Claire countered. ''I didn't do anything! You're the one's who's yelling!''

''I am not yelling!''

''You are, too, yelling!''

''I am not!''

''You are, too!''

''Am not!''

''Are, too!''

Haley let out a loud wail then, closing her eyes tight before cutting loose with a few more cries of sheer anguish. No matter what Nick did to try and soothe her, she wouldn't be calmed, and her wails grew louder still. In a last-ditch effort, he strode carefully over to Claire and held the baby out toward her.

At first Claire didn't understand what Nick was trying to do. Then her eyes widened as she realized he wanted her— *her*—to relieve him of the baby.

''Oh, no you don't,'' she said, taking an involuntary step backward. ''I can't calm her down. That's *your* job, Detective Daddy.''

''Yeah, well, I'm obviously not having any luck here,

Dr. Mommy," he pointed out unnecessarily. It was unnecessary, because Haley's howling intensified tenfold—and ten decibels—at least. "Maybe you'll do better with her."

"Don't count on it."

"Come on, Claire. You take the baby and calm her down, and I'll go make those phone calls."

It was a bribe, and she knew it, but it was effective in getting her to accept the baby from Nick, however reluctantly. Nevertheless, as soon as Claire tucked Haley into her arms—with only a minimal amount of juggling back and forth to get comfortable with her—the baby began to quiet some. Not a lot. But some.

Claire told herself it was doubtless only because the change of venue offered her some measure of distraction, and not because she herself was in any way suited to calming a fretful child. In spite of that, as she snuggled the baby closer and began to gently bounce her, the infant began to quiet even more.

"Okay," Claire murmured, to herself as much as to the baby. "We can do this. Yes, we can."

Nick disappeared the minute it was evident she had the baby in a reasonably good hold. She would have offered some parting shot at his hasty retreat, but she didn't want to risk upsetting the infant again.

Wow, she thought as she gazed down into a pair of huge, guileless eyes, seeming larger and more poignant, thanks to the presence of her unshed tears. It was amazing how these little creatures took over your entire life the minute they entered it—even the ones that didn't belong to you. Suddenly the whole universe seemed to revolve around one little bundle of flannel and diapers.

Since the baby's arrival on her doorstep, Claire hadn't been able to do one thing, or make one decision, or utter one word that didn't somehow involve the baby. No matter what she said or did, she'd had to think of the baby first. She and Nick had yet to have a conversation that didn't include some reference to the baby in some way.

Could this possibly be how it really was for new parents? Did babies honestly usurp this much of their time? Their thoughts? Their lives? She and Nick rarely even addressed the baby by name, she marveled further. They kept referring to Haley as "the baby," as if she were holy in some way, and speaking her name aloud would be tantamount to committing a profane act guaranteed to release the wrath of the gods.

Claire opened her mouth to test the theory, to utter Haley's name aloud. Then she hesitated, turning her gaze skyward, as if a lightning bolt might indeed rend her house in half, should she put voice to the child's name. Then, very quietly, very quickly, she said, "Haley."

All that happened in response was that the baby—Haley—made a small, contented little sound, then reached for a rhinestone button on Claire's shirt. She turned it right, then left, and smiled at the resultant sparkle of light that played in the stone. Claire waited a moment longer, but no angry lightning bolts descended, no roll of ominous thunder erupted and no angry gods made clear their displeasure. So, clearly, Haley wasn't—quite—of such supreme, divine importance.

Delighted by this turn of events, not to mention the baby's—or rather, Haley's—newly tranquil state of mind, Claire snuggled her a bit closer still. Okay, so maybe babies weren't all *that* bad, she conceded. As long as they belonged to someone else. As long as they were someone else's responsibility. As long as *she* didn't have to be the one who had to provide comfort and sustenance and support on a regular basis. This temporary arrangement was stressful enough. She couldn't imagine trying to do something like this on a permanent basis.

Thank God for Nick, she thought again. She wasn't sure how she would have managed this weekend without him.

But that thought, too, gradually ebbed away as Claire gazed down at Haley. She really was a sweetheart. This was the closest Claire had ever been to a baby before, and she had to confess now that she could kind of see the attraction, radioactive diapers or no. There was something about the way Haley fixed her gaze on Claire's face, so intently, as if she were trying to catalog every feature, attempting to understand just who this person holding her was, and what she was doing in Haley's life.

It occurred to Claire then that, in addition to Haley usurping her world and becoming the focal point thereof, she had likewise usurped Haley's world and become the focal point there. And she had to admit that there was something kind of nice about being a focal point, even for a baby. There was something kind of humbling and pleasurable in the knowledge that she was that important in another human being's life.

Yes, there was responsibility that came in caring for a child, but she saw now that that responsibility wasn't without its reward. For her trouble, Claire was receiving in return unconditional affection, and unconditional acceptance. And as rewards went, that was a pretty damned good one.

''What are we going to do with you?'' she asked Haley.

Haley glanced up from the button long enough to smile, and when she did, something inside Claire that had been clenched tight for a long, long time slowly began to unfold. Something that had been chilly slowly began to grow warm. And something that had been cowering suddenly began to calm.

''I guess you are pretty cute,'' she said softly, skimming

her hand lightly over the baby's comical hairdo. "But then, you already knew that, didn't you?"

Haley chuckled like an elf, then smiled in a way that revealed one sweet dimple on her plump little cheek. As much as Claire had tried to defend the baby's mother over the last several hours, she really couldn't imagine what would spur someone to surrender such a wonderful little girl to the care of a total stranger.

Then again, maybe Claire wasn't a total stranger.

She didn't know what made her think that, but somehow, once the thought appeared in her head, she couldn't quite make it go away. Maybe she had some unwitting relationship or connection to Haley's mother. She was an OB-GYN, after all, and certainly no stranger to pregnant women.

Could Haley's mother have been one of Claire's patients? she thought. She hadn't gotten a good look at the young woman, and there were hundreds of women visiting her offices at any given time. There were, after all, five women doctors practicing there. And patients who were expecting were required to see each of the doctors at least once at some point during their pregnancies, because it might be any of the five—frequently whichever of them was on call—who performed the actual delivery, once the patient's time came. The doctors wanted to be sure they had at least a vague acquaintance with each of the patients who was pregnant.

So in that regard, Claire may have very well met Haley's mother at some point, even if she were seen regularly by one of the other OB-GYNs in the practice. She might even be one of Claire's regular patients. She wracked her brain, trying to recall any young women with long, blond hair, but none came to mind off the top of her head.

Still, a check of the files might offer some revelation.

Nick had said Haley was about six months old or so. One of the clerical workers could check the files back that far to see who among their patients had delivered around that time, and if any fit the description of the young woman Claire had seen in her front yard the night before. Unfortunately, no one would be in the office this weekend to perform such a check. Whichever doctor was on call—Marian Hudson, if Claire remembered correctly—would be working from her home or making rounds at the hospital. And with the snow, the office would be difficult to reach.

But tomorrow it might be worth a shot.

She turned to go find Nick, to see what he thought of her powers of deductive reasoning, easily shifting the baby to her shoulder as she left the room. Haley immediately tangled both fists in the ponytail Claire had secured at the top of her head, drawing the long, straight tresses toward her mouth.

"Oh, no you don't," Claire said with a chuckle, tugging her hair free from the baby's grasp. "I'm on to you now, kiddo. And I just washed my hair. I am *not* going to take another shower today."

She shifted the baby once more, until her hair was safe from wandering little fingers, so once again Haley contented herself with the buttons on Claire's shirt. Amazing how the world must seem through such new eyes, Claire thought. Things she herself didn't even notice anymore became intriguing and fascinating to the inquisitive investigation of a very young child.

She found Nick downstairs in her office with a phone pressed to one ear. He was leaning back in *her* desk chair, with *his* feet propped up on *her* desk as he played computer solitaire while chatting with whomever was on the other end of the line. She shook her head ruefully at how quickly and thoroughly he'd made himself comfortable in her home.

Something about his familiarity, however, struck a warm chord inside her. Why shouldn't he make himself at home? she thought. Had things turned out differently, this might very well be his home.

Immediately, ruthlessly, she reminded herself again that things *hadn't* turned out differently, then took a moment to berate herself further for the way she kept forgetting that. Even if, by some wild miracle, the two of them got back together after all this time, Nick would still want to start a family right away. And he'd want Claire to stay at home and care for that family. Which meant she'd be expected to give up her practice, to simply forego all those years of college and residency, to sacrifice the entire life she'd built for herself in the last several years.

And since there was no way they'd be able to afford this house on Nick's salary as a detective, *neither* of them would be calling this place home for long. They'd end up doing as Nick had always wanted—they'd buy a small house to raise their large family, then scrimp and save and sacrifice to make sure their kids had all the basic necessities.

Though, when she thought about it, Claire realized it wasn't the scrimping and saving and small house she would mind in such a scenario. She really wasn't materialistic, in spite of the expensive things she'd acquired over the years. No, what she minded in Nick's plan for their future was the loss of her work. It wasn't selfishness on her part that made her crave employment. She simply knew she could never be completely happy without it. Being a doctor was a much a part of her as being a mother would be. And she didn't see why she should have to sacrifice her career in order to become a mom.

And now that she thought more about it, she didn't see why she should have to sacrifice motherhood in order to have her career. There were plenty of women who juggled both roles successfully, plenty of women who managed to work jobs they loved, and raise happy kids in the process. Then again, why was it always the mother who was expected to do it all? To have it all? How come nobody ever figured the father into the equation?

Then again, she didn't even *want* to be a mother, so what was the point in having this discussion with herself?

Her thoughts were thankfully scattered when Nick hung up the phone and spun around in his chair. He sighed heavily and lifted both hands to his eyes, knuckling them gently before scrubbing his palms over his rough jaws. He may have showered and changed, but he hadn't shaved, and now the lower half of his face was darkened by more than a day's growth of beard. Faint purple crescents had formed under his dark eyes, and his hair was a mess, as if he'd spent most of his time on the telephone with one hand tangled uneasily in the thick tresses.

He just looked so adorably rumpled, Claire thought. So sweetly exhausted. So sexily domestic. Not for the first time since seeing him on the other side of her front door, Claire was nearly overrun by memories of how the two of them had been together once upon a time. And she was nearly overwhelmed by the strong physical attraction she still felt for him. Had it not been for the baby who was plucking at her buttons and drooling on her shirt, Claire might very well have done something in that moment that she would have doubtless lived to regret.

Like rush into his arms and pull him close. Like press her mouth to his and kiss him for all she was worth. Like tumble him to the floor and have her way with him. Over and over and over again.

She hadn't been with many men since Nick, but even the few with whom she'd dared brave intimacy hadn't measured up to him at all. There had been none of the fire, none of the intensity, none of the sheer, unadulterated *need* that had always been present whenever she and Nick had come together.

There had been none of the emotion, either. None of the love. For that reason, her few relationships with other men since Nick had been short-lived. And for that reason, it had been quite some time since she'd been intimate with anyone. She tallied the months, the years, mentally...

Oh, no, surely it couldn't be *that* long, she thought. Then again, maybe that would explain why her desire had leapt so quickly and completely to the fore, simply by having Nick present in her home. Of course, that could also have happened just because she'd never stopped wanting him.

Had never stopped loving him.

Oh, why had it been he who had been sent to respond to her call? she asked herself for perhaps the hundredth time since he had arrived. Of all the luck...

"No luck," he said, dropping his hands into his lap. "I tried all the people I couldn't reach last night, and a few more I thought of in the meantime. But either nobody's answering their phone, or else they can't get through the snow or they have something a lot more important to see to than an abandoned baby."

Claire gaped at him. "What on earth could be more important than an abandoned baby?" she demanded, feeling strangely protective of Haley for some reason. How dare anyone suggest that she wasn't of the utmost consequence in the whole, wide world.

Nick shrugged. "Gee, I don't know, Claire. Murder. Arson. Drugs. Even your garden-variety mayhem seems to take precedence here."

"That's outrageous," she said indignantly.

She told herself she was only championing Haley's welfare because no one else would, and *not* because of any personal feelings she might be developing for the little cherub. She *wasn't* developing any personal feelings for Haley. Well, none other than that one that thought the baby was just really, really cute. And really, really sweet. And really, really adorable. And really, really wonderful. But that was the only one.

"There must be someone out there who knows what to do," she added, involuntarily snuggling Haley closer.

"Social Services usually handles this kind of thing," Nick said. "But it's tough to reach anybody on the weekends. Add this weather into the mix, and you're just going to have to accept the fact that things aren't going to get done as well as they usually do. We should have more luck tomorrow. It'll be back to the regular workweek, and by then, some of this snow should be cleared and/or melted away."

Claire sighed heavily, defeatedly, and turned her gaze to the window. "At least it's finally stopped snowing."

"And according to The Weather Channel, it's supposed to be warming up this afternoon quite a bit," Nick threw in. "Every little bit will help. In the meantime, I think we have enough diapers and food for the baby, so she shouldn't run low."

Claire dropped her gaze down to the baby's face, only to find Haley gazing back at her with what appeared to be rather sleepy interest. "Do you think it's too early to put her down for a nap? She looks kind of tired."

Nick shrugged. He sure looked as though *he* could use a nap, she thought. "Hard to say without knowing what her usual routine is," he said.

Routine. Claire wanted to laugh at the word. Had it only

been yesterday that she had been enjoying a routine in her own life? Of course, that routine had been somewhat, well…routine. In other words, boring. But at least it had been something familiar, something predictable, something comforting.

Oh, all right, and something boring, too. But it had been *her* boring routine. And she'd worked hard to earn it. Having it disrupted to the extent that it had been unsettled her in ways she really didn't want to investigate. Mainly because she was pretty sure Nick was an integral part of her…unsettlement.

Haley yawned hugely, and Claire couldn't help laughing. She was just so cute. So sweet. How could Claire have not known this about babies before?

"I think she needs a nap," she said softly.

"Fine," Nick told her. "Why don't you take her upstairs and rock her for a while?"

Claire waited for the panic that she knew would accompany Nick's suggestion, but oddly, it barely made a squeak inside her this time. "Okay," she said, turning toward the office door. "If you're sure you'll be okay down here."

"I'm sure."

Something in his voice made her turn around, and something in his expression made her pause. He looked like a man who was plotting something, but for the life of her Claire couldn't imagine what. With a man like Nick, though, if he *was* plotting something…?

Well, it could only lead to no good.

Putting that thought aside—for now—Claire turned again and made her way back toward the stairs.

Seven

Nick may have preferred Bruce Springsteen for his lullabies, but Claire was much more a traditionalist in that respect. And really, when all was said and done, Haley fell asleep just as quickly and easily to "Stairway to Heaven" as she had to The Boss. So that just went to show how much Nick *really* knew about this baby stuff. Claire could teach him a thing or two.

She marveled at that thought as it unfolded in her head, then gazed down at the baby who was snoozing so peacefully in her lap. Claire teaching Nick something about babies. Now there was a shocking development. Had anyone told her twelve years ago—or even twelve hours ago—that she would be successfully rocking a baby to sleep one day, Claire would have guffawed right in their face. True, she'd never really had the opportunity—or the inclination, for that matter—to learn, but now that she'd been forced into the position of caretaker to abandoned infants, she had to admit that, maybe, perhaps, possibly…

…she'd been wrong about them.

Wrong. Now that was something to think about. Okay, so maybe it was as hard for Claire to admit to being…wrong…as it was for Nick Campisano. Maybe she had been as stubborn back then as he had been. She'd demanded a career, and she hadn't been willing to compromise on that in any way, shape or form. But the reason she had wanted a career was because she honestly hadn't thought there would ever be anything else for her. She hadn't thought she would be happy being a wife and mother. She hadn't thought she would be happy with anyone, in the long run, except herself and Nick. And she had been positive that Nick wouldn't want her unless she became his wife and the mother of his children.

And she had been right.

But now that all she had was her career and herself, she was beginning to wonder how wise she had been all those years ago, to be so certain of her future. True, she had no desire to give up either—not her job, not herself. Not for kids. And not even for Nick. She just couldn't make such huge sacrifices and still remain a full, happy human being.

Then again, she wasn't a full, happy human being now, either, she realized, even with her career and herself. So what exactly *did* she have? Not much, she had to confess. Not beyond a few material possessions that brought her dubious satisfaction. She wasn't entirely happy. She wasn't entirely fulfilled. Things between her and Nick were no more settled now than they had been twelve years ago. And likewise, there wasn't much more hope of a resolution now than there had been then. They were both still stubborn, still uncertain, still unwilling to bend.

They were *both* unhappy. They were *both* unfulfilled.

And, evidently, they were *both* destined to remain that way unless they could reach some kind of compromise. But what each of them wanted *couldn't* be compromised. Claire's job demanded too much of her. And Nick demanded children.

Oh, why did it always have to come back to that? she wondered. Why did this seem so hard, when it should be so simple? They'd never stopped loving each other. They still wanted each other. They could probably make each other happy. So why did it all seem so impossible? Coming to a compromise shouldn't be this difficult. But she could see no way to make it work, because her needs and Nick's were so irreconcilable.

Haley looked so peaceful and sweet, sound asleep as she was, that for a long time, Claire could only continue rocking slowly, humming softly under her breath, watching her. The tiny fingers of one hand were wrapped loosely around Claire's thumb, while her other hand was fisted over her lap. Her dark hair shot straight up like corn silk, and fine blue veins were threaded beneath her perfect, ivory skin. Beneath Claire's own hand, she could feel the minute pulsing of the baby's heart, and she watched the subtle rise and fall of Haley's chest as she slumbered more deeply.

She was a tiny, lap-size miracle. A minuscule bundle of raw potential. A human being who would grow and develop and learn and live. And Claire realized then, with no small amount of dismay, that she didn't want to let her go.

"Oh, boy," she whispered on an uneven sigh.

When had this happened? she wondered. And what on earth was she going to do about it?

Pushing the questions aside for now, she stood carefully and returned Haley to the basket on the floor by her bed. Then slowly she pivoted on her heel to leave, and wasn't quite surprised to find Nick standing in the doorway, watching her. Leaning against the doorjamb, his hands pushed deep into denim pockets, he appeared to have been standing there for some time. And from the look on his face, his thoughts weren't too far off the mark from Claire's own. It was clear that he knew what she'd been thinking about as she watched Haley sleep, that he knew what she'd been hoping for, what she'd been wanting to happen.

She waited for him to murmur a smug *I told you so.* But he said not a word as she approached him, just maneuvered himself backward and to the side so that she could pass him and make her way into the hall. She pulled the door closed behind her very slowly, halting when a scant inch of space separated it from the frame. And then, without thinking about or questioning what she was doing, she dipped her forehead into Nick's chest and nestled her whole body against his.

He hesitated for only an instant, as if her action had caught him completely off guard. Then, immediately after that instant, he wrapped his arms around her, firmly, possessively, lovingly, and pulled her deep into his embrace. Beneath her ear, she heard the steady *thump-thump-thump* of his heartbeat pulse reassuringly, its pace increasing ever so slightly when she snuggled deeper still. He smelled of her soap, and her shampoo and her sheets, and something about that made him seem as if he were indeed a part of her. The warmth and solid strength of him surrounded her, as it had so often, so many years ago, and in that moment, Claire let herself forget everything that had passed in the space of time that had separated them.

In that moment, she let herself be swayed by her memories of him, and her dreams of him, by her need for him, and her love for him. And when he curled a finger under her chin and tipped her head back to meet his gaze, she didn't even try to hide her feelings. For a moment they

only stood there gazing at each other, longing for each
other, needing each other. Then slowly, slowly…oh, so
slowly…Nick lowered his head to hers and covered
Claire's mouth with his own.

He tasted exactly the way that she remembered him, full
of heat and life and an easygoing spirit. He was everything
she'd always wanted to find in a mate, everything she'd
never quite been herself. He was, as he had always been,
her perfect complement—physically, emotionally, spiritu-
ally. His body fit to hers as if they were joined as one, and
he filled all the empty places inside of her that no one else
had come close to even reaching. As he deepened his kiss,
Claire felt as if she was finally returning home after being
gone too long on an unpleasant, exhaustive voyage.

She melted into him, into his kiss, curving her fingers
over his shoulders, pushing herself up on tiptoe so that she
might facilitate the experience for them both. Nick needed
no further encouragement. He opened his mouth wider, explored her more intimately, pulled her body flush against
his own. And Claire went willingly, hopefully, disregarding
the warning bells that were barely tinkling in the very back
of her brain…faintly, like beautiful glass wind chimes.

Boy, some alarm system she had.

And then even that thought evaporated, to be replaced
by a wealth of sensation that she hadn't felt for a very long
time. Twelve years, to be exact. The last time she'd found
herself in the arms of Nick Campisano.

Nothing had changed, she realized. Nothing. He was still
big and strong and firm and fit. He still filled her lungs with
a mix of spice and wind and musk and man. His body still
felt warm and hard beneath her fingertips. He still
tasted…oh, so wonderful. She might very well have been
twenty-two again, she mused vaguely. Because that was
exactly how he made her feel.

She urged her body up more, thrusting her entire torso against his, then roped her arms around his neck and threaded the fingers of both hands through his thick, silky hair. Nick came to her willingly, looping his own arms around her waist, spreading his fingers open over her back to push her higher toward himself. He deepened their kiss even more, thrusting his tongue inside her mouth for a thorough taste of her, then turned them so that she was leaning back against the wall. He arced one arm over her head, flattened the other against the wall near her shoulder and crowded his entire body against hers.

Claire found herself trapped between the cool, ungiving wall behind her and Nick's hot, unyielding body before her, and the sense of his overwhelming possession thrilled her in a way that nothing else could. With one hand still entwined in his hair, she dropped the other open over the soft fabric of the sweatshirt that stretched taut across his chest. As she grazed her open palm over him, she felt the rigid ripple of every poetic muscle, the unapologetic raging of his heart. Then he swooped in more, tilting his head to one side to carry the kiss further, and ground his pelvis against hers. And she felt then how ripe and ready he was for her.

But evidently even that flagrant intimacy wasn't enough for Nick, because he dropped his hand from the wall and curved his fingers over her rib cage, opening his hand until he—almost—cradled the lower curve of her breast between his thumb and fingers. For a moment, he didn't proceed further, only pressed his hand intimately against her, rubbing the soft fabric of her shirt up and down along her rib cage, each tentative caress singeing her sensitive flesh. Then slowly he inched his hand upward, bit by bit, until he covered her breast completely.

At her ragged expulsion of breath, he hesitated, then started to pull away. So Claire covered his hand with hers and dragged it back to where he had laid it. Nick pulled his head back from hers when she did, not to withdraw from her, but to gaze down at the sight of their hands folded together over her breast. His cheeks were stained with the flush of his desire, his eyes were dark with his need. But he didn't alter his gaze as he closed his hand tightly over her breast, even when Claire groaned aloud her satisfaction with his gesture.

She started to remove her hand from his, to give Nick free rein, but he softly murmured, "No. Do it with me, Claire."

She hesitated a moment, surprised by his suggestion, then cupped her hand over the back of his again. He moved his fingers aside, linking their hands loosely together, so that she was touching herself, too. Then he led them both in a path of erotic exploration that left her dizzy and intoxicated. Before she realized what he was doing, he flicked open the top button of her shirt, then the next and the next, pushing the fabric over her shoulder to expose the champagne-colored lace of her brassiere beneath. Then he flicked the front closure of that open, as well, and bared her breast to the warm air surrounding them.

He moved their hands to the naked mound of flesh, and Claire didn't think she'd ever felt anything so exquisite in her life as their joint caresses. Nick's breathing, like her own, became ragged and irregular, his body temperature reaching a fever heat, just as her own did. She tipped her head back until the wall prevented her from going any further, an action that left her neck exposed for Nick's eager invasion.

After one warm nuzzle, he opened his damp mouth over the slender column of her throat, then dragged the tip of his tongue down to the delicate hollow at its base. From there, he rubbed his lips over her collarbone, down her breastbone, until he hovered near the fully bloomed peak of her breast. Drawing her nipple deeply into his mouth, Nick sucked hard, laving her with the flat of his tongue, tickling her with the tip.

Claire groaned again, her entire body going limp. Then she curled her fingers tightly in his dark hair. After freeing the remainder of her buttons, Nick pushed her shirt completely open, leaving her bra to dangle from her shoulders like willow branches in a breeze. He filled both hands with her breasts, squeezing them together, tasting first one and then the other, then back and forth again. And whichever wasn't in his mouth was in his firm grasp—he toyed with her expertly, teased her to a frenzy, sparked a fire inside her that threatened to burn out of control.

"Oh," Claire murmured. "Oh, Nick."

Okay, so maybe one thing had changed, she thought vaguely. Nick was quite a bit more…*insistent*…and…*thorough*…in his technique these days. Not that he'd ever been a clumsy lover by any stretch of the imagination, but he'd obviously matured in more ways than one over the last twelve years. When they were kids, their lovemaking had been intense and hot. But it had also been pretty short-lived and conventional. Do that, touch this, then he was spilling himself inside her. She was beginning to realize that, over the years, Nick had had an opportunity to learn a few new tricks.

And she tried not to dwell on the fact that he'd learned them from someone else.

No time for such thoughts now, she told herself. All that mattered was the here and now. The two of them and the way they were—not then, but now. Now. *Now.*

"Now," she said aloud, fairly gasping the word.

But Nick seemed not to hear her, so focused was he on other things. He'd caught one nipple between thumb and

forefinger and rolled it gently around, while still consuming
the other with thirsty, insistent demand. Instinctively Claire
dropped her hands to the hem of his sweatshirt and began
to push it higher, up over the ripple of rock-hard abs, up
over the rich dark hair scattered across his chest and belly.
Nick stopped what he was doing long enough for her to
shove the garment up over his head and toss it aside, then
he dove in again to consume her.

As he bent forward, Claire pressed her mouth to his hot,
naked shoulder, pulling her tongue along the musky satin
of his skin. The taste of salt and sweat and male animal
only served to enflame her desire for him, and unable to
help herself, she nipped him lightly with her teeth.

Okay, so maybe Nick wasn't the only one who'd devel-
oped a few new maneuvers over the years, she thought with
some satisfaction when he yelped and straightened. For a
moment, he said nothing, only stared at her in openmouthed
shock. Then slowly he smiled with utter delight.

"You animal," he said.

"Woof," she replied with a grin.

His smile fell some, though, as he swept his gaze down
the length of her entire, half-clad body, then back up again.
Claire could only imagine what she must look like with
her clothes in such disarray and her desire for him raging
so clearly. Probably exactly what he looked like with *his*
clothes in such disarray and his desire for *her* raging so
clearly.   Wow. She must look pretty damned hot.

"I want you," he said simply.

She swallowed hard. "I want you, too."

"No, Claire, I mean I *want* you. All of you. Every last
inch of you. I want to be deep inside you, and I want to
make it last. A long, *long* time."

She inhaled a lengthy, fortifying breath at the out-and-out demand in his voice, then released it as evenly as she could. "Sounds good to me," she managed to say. But her voice was soft and tremulous as she spoke.

Nick seemed not to notice, because he only nodded slowly and took a step forward, resuming his previous posture, one arm arced over her head, his entire body pressed into hers. With her bare breasts molded against the heated steel of his chest, the soft hair prickled her sensitive flesh. She nearly wept with the exquisite sharpness of the sensation. Then Nick dropped his free hand to her thigh, moved it easily forward, then scraped his fingers upward, settling them at the damp juncture of her legs.

"Oh," she said, the sound a scant whisper in the silent hall. "Oh, that's…"

She never finished what she was going to say, because he flicked a long finger against her, rubbed it deep between her legs, and Claire nearly came undone. Her knees suddenly buckled beneath her, but he'd pressed himself against her so tightly, that her body moved not an inch. When he realized what was happening to her, he grinned with *much* satisfaction, then scooped her up in his arms and covered the few steps necessary to bring them both inside the room he had claimed the night before. He didn't put her down until he stood beside the bed, and even then he followed her right down onto the mattress.

Instinctively she opened to him as he lay atop and alongside her, shrugging out of her shirt and bra as he pushed both from her shoulders. Freed of the garments, she reached for the zipper on his blue jeans and tugged it down, flipping the button open easily and scooting her hand deep inside both his jeans and briefs.

She found him effortlessly, as if her fingers had known exactly where to go. He was well-remembered, well-loved territory, and Claire caressed him over and over and over again. Oh, he felt so good in her hand. She fitted her palm over the head of his shaft, sliding it over the dampness of his ready desire for her. Nick rolled to his back and lay still, but his breathing was labored and thready. She removed her hand and shoved his garments down around his hips, then, feeling more wanton than she'd ever felt in her life, she curled up her body beside him and bent her head toward him.

"Oh, Claire," he said. "You never...before...oh..."

No, she never had before. But for some reason, nothing made her happier now than performing this gesture for Nick. It was the ultimate intimacy, and she needed for him to know how very much she loved him. So she opened her mouth over him and took him inside.

He tangled his fingers in her hair as she laved and loved him, tugging free the band wound around it so that her hair cascaded around her face and him both. Then, after winding a few errant tresses in his hands, he lay so still, she began to wonder if he was entirely unaffected by her motions. Braving a glance up at his face, she saw that he had his eyes closed, his lips parted, as if her were perched at the edge of madness. Moving her mouth up and down along his hard length once more, Claire nuzzled the dark fur of his belly, tasted his navel, then toured back up to his throat.

Before she could reach his mouth, however, Nick, with a surprising show of strength and animation, deftly maneuvered her onto her back. "Your turn," he said as he reached for the waistband of her leggings. After he'd shed them, with his blue jeans still open, his member straining to reach its mate, he pushed Claire onto her back and positioned himself between her legs to feast upon her.

It was...oh...such exquisite torture, such forbidden delight. The heat of his breath and the dampness of his mouth dancing over that most sensitive part of her provided a sensation unlike anything she'd ever experienced before. Over and over Nick pleasured her, plowed her, penetrated her, until she didn't think she could tolerate any more. Then, just when she was certain she would burst into flame, she felt him move again, this time away from her. When she opened her eyes, he stood beside the bed, stepping out of the last of his clothes.

"Roll over," he told her, his smile mischievous.

A tiny explosion detonated in her stomach, heating her entire body. "Why?" she asked breathlessly.

"I want to try something a little…different."

She arched her brows in surprise. "What do you call what we just did?"

His smile turned lascivious. "It's a day of discovery. Roll over."

Still not sure what he had planned, Claire rolled to her side, giving him her back. She felt the mattress dip behind her as Nick rejoined her, then the press of his long body aligning itself with hers. She glanced back over her shoulder to find him eyeing her backside with much affection, then he curved a hand over her naked hip and skimmed it down along her thigh.

"You are so beautiful, Claire," he murmured reverentially. "Your body has changed over the years."

She couldn't quite prevent the derisive chuckle his comment aroused. "Yeah, tell me about it. I've gained fifteen pounds since college."

"You wear it well. You're so much more…more lush and round and soft."

"That's the problem," she concurred.

He shook his head. "It's arousing as hell is what it is."

Before she could protest his observation, he dragged his hand back up to her hip, then down to her fanny, where he cupped one half of her bottom. She felt so vulnerable with her back to him this way, but so confident of his love for her, that the two feelings entwined to create another, more shadowy sensation inside. He moved his hand lower, between her legs, then lifted one and draped it back over his own thigh. He looped an arm over her waist, then reached up to mold his hand over her breast. Then he dipped his head to her neck and kissed her gently.

"I'm assuming you've taken the proper precautions against pregnancy," he said.

She strove to hear some bitterness or sarcasm in his voice, but there was neither. Simply a statement of assumption, and an unspoken offer to take care of such a thing himself if she hadn't already.

She nodded. "I've been on the Pill for some time now." She waited to see if he would ask if that was because she was involved with someone else, and when he didn't, offered up an explanation herself. She needed for him to know. "Not because I've been seeing anyone," she said. "I haven't been. Not for a long time. It's been to help alleviate some of the problems I was having with my cycle."

He nodded against her shoulder. "Thanks for telling me. I haven't been involved with anyone for a long time, either."

Only when she knew the truth did Claire realize how much she had been bothered by the prospect of his being linked now to another woman. She rejoiced in the knowledge that they were both free and clear, then told herself it didn't matter, because there would be nothing for them after this weekend. Not unless one of them was willing to make a sacrifice neither seemed willing to concede.

"So you won't get pregnant then," he said, thankfully scattering her thoughts.

"I shouldn't," she corrected him, knowing that the method wasn't exactly foolproof.

"And that's good enough for you?"

She nodded, mildly surprised to realize that it was. "Yes," she said softly.

The hand on her thigh moved back between her legs again, and Nick parted her softly, gently, with sure fingers. Claire closed her eyes to sharpen the experience, then was nearly overwhelmed by the keenness of it all. For a moment, he only fondled her, creasing her damp folds, entering her with one long finger, then two, scraping the pad of his thumb delicately over the sensitive nub of her flesh. Then he shifted his big body again and entered her deeply from behind, burying himself completely inside her.

"Oh," she cried softly. "Oh, Nick. That's so…oh…"

Neither of them spoke a word after that. Claire reached behind herself to cup her hand over Nick's taut buttock, and she opened her legs wider to facilitate his entry. She caught his rhythm and matched it easily, moving her body backward as he thrust his own forward, the friction of their slick bodies magnifying the heat of their desire. As they climbed higher and higher, their need to cry out multiplied, but neither succumbed, for fear of waking Haley. So in silence, Nick bucked forward one final time, pressing both hands flat over her belly to push her backward against him. She nestled her bottom against him, reveling in the spill of his passion deep inside her.

For a long moment, they lay joined motionlessly, then Nick withdrew and rolled Claire onto her back and covered her body with his. He propped himself up on his elbows, so as not to crush her, then cupped her face in his hands and kissed her deeply, resolutely, as if he were branding her his, once and for all. Then he rolled onto his own back and pulled her with him, curling one arm around her shoulders, dropping the other to her opposite hip.

And when Claire would have spoken aloud, he hastily lifted his hand again and softly pressed a finger to her lips, to prevent her from uttering a word.

''Later,'' he said. ''We'll talk later. Right now...''

He never finished whatever he wanted to say, but somehow Claire knew exactly what he meant. Later, she told herself. They would talk later.

Eight

They lay holding each other silently for some time afterward, neither wanting to end what was sure to be all too temporary, Nick supposed. But it had been so long since he had been able to wrap his arms around Claire this way, so long since he had been able to feel as if he were genuinely a part of her—as she had become a part of him. And he had dreamed of this so many times, this closeness, this intimacy, that he simply had no desire to let her go. Ever.

Haley continued to sleep, and hadn't wakened during their lovemaking, even when their efforts to keep silent had been less than successful. Still, there had been something totally arousing about their efforts to keep quiet, and in the denial to give free rein to their desires. Of course, it only caused Nick to want to make love to Claire again—right away—but he was hesitant to surrender this peaceful moment just yet.

The feel of her warm, soft, naked body stretched out

along his own was something he'd feared he would never experience again, and having her close in such a way now was just too wonderful to end. Her legs were twined easily with his, and his pelvis half cradled hers as she lay on her stomach alongside and atop him. She had folded one arm over his belly and twined her fingers in the dark hair scattered across his chest. One breast was flattened against his torso, the other against his ribs, and he could feel the rapid pulsing of her heartbeat slowing gradually along with his own.

In so many ways, they seemed to be one being, one individual right now. Yet, in so many ways, he knew, that would never be possible. They each wanted too much for a future that was too different from what the other envisioned. And neither seemed willing to concede even an inch. Truth be told, Nick was more than willing to talk compromise these days. But just how could they compromise something like Claire's career, to which she'd devoted years of education, residency and work in setting up her practice? How could they compromise something like his own desire to have a passel of kids, when he wanted so much to make children—his children—a part of his life?

He had thought that making love with Claire would mend all the loose, ragged pieces their lives had become over the years. He had thought if they could just recapture what they had once had, they would both realize how much each was missing, and reach out to take what was rightfully theirs. He had thought that in acknowledging how very much they needed each other, they would both be forced to confront what they simply could not deny any longer.

He had thought that making love to Claire would make everything right.

But instead of simplifying things, making love had only complicated their relationship more thoroughly. And now the silence between them stretched longer, more taut, until he knew one of them had to say something to ease it. So, even though he was the one who had requested the quiet, Nick took the initiative and voiced what was first and foremost in his mind at the moment.

"I love you," he said simply, uncertain when he'd chosen to speak those precise words aloud, but having no desire to take them back once uttered. Nevertheless, he couldn't quite make himself look down at Claire, wasn't quite sure her response would mirror his own. So he only gazed up at the ceiling, studying the play of light there that was refracted through the ice lacing the windowpanes. "I have loved you for so long," he added carefully. "I never once stopped, you know?"

At first she said nothing in response to his avowal, but the fingers that had been dancing lightly across his chest halted, hovering over his heart. She lay still and silent for some moments, then, without looking up at him, and very, very quietly, she said, "Nick, I'm not sure this is something we should be—"

"You can't tell me this is news to you," he interrupted, not wanting to hear any objection from her, even though he'd known her reaction would be one of protest.

She sighed heavily, laid her palm open flat over his heart and murmured, "No. No, it's not news to me."

Nick heartened some, then cursed himself for even feeling slightly optimistic. "Then why shouldn't we talk about it?" he demanded quietly.

Again she hesitated for a long time before answering. Finally she said, "Because…because being with you again is so sudden, and so unexpected, and the situation is strange, to say the least, and it came out of nowhere, and I'm not sure we can trust what we're feeling right now, and there's—"

"I can trust my feelings," he interjected confidently. "I can trust my feelings just fine. I know *exactly* how I feel, Claire."

She tilted her head back to look up at him, and Nick bent his own to meet her gaze. "Then you're a better man than I," she told him. "Because I'm nowhere close to knowing exactly what I feel at the moment."

Reluctantly he yielded. For now. "You don't have to say anything," he told her. "You don't have to tell me how you feel."

Her expression grew faintly puzzled. "I don't?"

He shook his head. "I already know how you feel."

Now her expression became doubtful. "Do you?" she asked. "Do you really?"

He nodded, but he couldn't quite bring himself to put voice to his conviction—it wasn't something he wanted to hear spoken aloud. Claire did love him. Of that he was absolutely certain. She couldn't possibly have responded to him the way she had just responded if she didn't still love him the way she had all those years ago. Problem was, though, she hadn't loved him *enough* back then. And she still didn't. Love him enough.

Somehow, though, even acknowledging that fact didn't totally dishearten Nick. He tightened the arm he had wrapped around her shoulder, and pulled her closer, tangling his fingers in her hair, kissing the crown of her head.

"It doesn't matter," he lied. "All that matters right now is that we're here together like this. Who knows how much time we have together? Let's take advantage of it while we can."

Nick, of course, had intended for that to mean they should make love again—right away—but Claire evidently had an entirely different interpretation of his comment.

Likewise, she evidently had something entirely different on her mind.

"Nick, do you like being a cop?" she asked quietly.

Gee, nothing like a question straight out of left field to mess with a guy's amorous mood. "Yeah," he answered automatically, as he always did when posed such a question. "I like being a cop a lot. I never wanted to be anything else—you know that. Why do you ask?"

He felt, more than saw her shrug, but she began to dance her fingers lightly over his chest again, something he took to be a good sign for more potential hanky-panky in the not-too-distant future. She also shifted her leg a bit, moving it more intimately between his, and he decided that yes, this was definitely a good sign. At least, it had damned well better be a good sign, because with that one subtle nudge, she had driven him to rousing life again.

"I don't know why," she told him. "I just wondered. Seems like being a narcotics detective would be pretty stressful. And the way you feel about kids... I don't know. Seems like it might be kind of disillusioning sometimes to keep seeing kids in trouble the way you do."

"Yeah, it can be," he conceded. "Sometimes. But it's probably no more stressful than doing what you do."

She glanced up at him again, her clear concern darkening her eyes. "Yeah, but I never have to put my life in danger," she pointed out. "I'm never out there face to face with people who are heavily armed and completely amoral or, worse, strung out on something that makes their behavior totally unpredictable and irrational and dangerous."

He forced a smile, hoping to alleviate some of her fears, even though they were fears that mirrored his own sometimes. "Hey, I've been around my sisters and sisters-in-law when they're pregnant," he told her. "Talk about unpredictable and irrational behavior, never mind *dangerous*..."

She poked him playfully in the ribs, but he could see that she wasn't pacified. "I mean it, Nick. What you do *is* dangerous. And what you see sometimes has got to mess with your ideals. How do you stand it?"

This time he was the one to shrug, even though what Claire said was exactly true. His job did mess with his ideals. Big-time. So much so that there were times when Nick didn't think he had any ideals left. Who could hope for the best when what you saw everyday was the dark, rank underbelly of the human animal? Who could look for the good in people when the behavior you saw as a routine part of your job was despicable and loathsome and mean? Who could keep on trying to help others, when it seemed like every hand extended in aid got clawed bloody or bitten off?

When he thought back on the kind of man he had been when he'd first been bumped up to detective, he had to laugh. Or, rather, he would have laughed—if there had been anything funny in what he'd witnessed over the years. Seven years ago, Nick had been the kind of man who had honestly seen hope for the future. He'd genuinely thought he could make a difference in kids' lives. He had sincerely believed he could be instrumental in effecting change for the better.

Hah. What a laugh. In seven years' time, he'd seen no improvement at all.

"I don't know how I stand it," he said softly, forced to glance away from the earnest worry he saw etched on her face. "I just try not to think about that part of it."

"Then what part *do* you think about?"

He returned his gaze to the ceiling, but this time he saw something other than the play of sunlight dappled there. "I think about the kids who *aren't* using," he said. "I think about how important it is to get this stuff off the streets, so no more kids get hurt or sick or killed. I think about turning the kids on to other things that would keep them off drugs—sports, school, religion, whatever. I think about all the programs we cops have initiated over the years to help kids deal with the problems they have, and to help keep other kids from getting into drugs in the first place. I think about how I'm trying to make a difference in some of their lives.''

He paused, inhaled deeply and released the breath in a long, ragged, thoughtful sigh. ''And then something happens that makes me have to think about how miserably we're failing in all those areas.''

It was true, he admitted to himself. No matter how hard they tried to attack the drug problem, it never went away. It never even got smaller. For every kid they helped, three more got lost. For every new program they introduced in the hopes of offering aid or prevention, two old programs got axed for being ineffective or underfunded. They employed more cops in narcotics now than they ever had before, but the drug problem was bleeding faster than they could staunch it. At this rate, Nick thought, it would be no time at all before they were all calling it quits.

''So, then, I guess you'll just have to work harder, won't you?'' Claire said quietly.

He told himself to agree with her, to at least nod his acceptance of that fact. Problem was, it was getting harder and harder for him to roll out of bed and go to work in the morning. It was getting harder and harder for him to dress up like a dealer or a buyer and play a role he despised. It was getting harder and harder not to have contempt for the very people he'd been trying so hard to help for years. And it was getting harder and harder to have any real feeling of worth for what he was doing.

"Yeah," he muttered. "I guess I'll just have to work harder."

He reached for Claire again, wanting nothing more than to lose himself in her for even a few more minutes. And she, clearly sensing his need for her, rolled her body over onto his, then pushed herself up to brush his lips with her own. He had filled her mouth with his tongue, had cupped her taut, tight fanny with both hands and was spreading her legs open over his thighs when he heard Haley rousing in the room across the hall. As irritated as he was by the intrusion, the soft sound made him smile. It also flooded completely any burning desire he might have been entertaining for Claire.

"Sounds like we're being summoned," he said.

She chuckled. "And gosh, isn't her timing just perfect."

"Exactly what it should be for a baby," he said.

With one brief, final kiss, Claire pushed herself away from him, and Nick couldn't stop looking at her as she rose from the bed. For a moment, it was as if they'd never been apart, as if she were rising from wherever they'd managed to sneak away to make love—the banks of Greenmeadow Creek, or the back seat of his Chevy Nova, or one of those brief, sweet times they'd sprung for a hotel. Every now and then, they'd stolen an afternoon in Claire's bed while her parents were at work, their hearts beating double time, their passion enflamed, over the possibility of being discovered there.

No such threats existed now, and Nick still felt as randy as a teenager. How the hell was he supposed to continue on with his life after this weekend with Claire? How was he supposed to make it through each day without seeing her? Without touching her? Without making love to her? There was no way he could go back to living without her.

But what were the chances of living with her, as long as things stood between them the way they did now?

When Haley's cries from the next room grew more insistent, Claire hastened her dressing. She was still buttoning up her shirt when she exited, and only then did Nick realize he still lay in bed naked. That naturally led to his realization that it had been Claire—and not he—who had responded to Haley's needs. And *that,* he decided, was a very interesting development.

Claire had automatically taken it upon herself, had instinctively been the one, to go and see to Haley. She wasn't terrified of the baby anymore. Imagine that.

So if she wasn't terrified of Haley, then maybe, just maybe, she wouldn't be terrified of the prospect of having one or two—or six—of her own. Well, well, well. One hurdle crossed.

Not so fast, Campisano, he cautioned himself. Just because Claire wasn't panicking over someone else's kid didn't mean she had her own womb for rent. There was a big difference between liking kids and wanting kids. Still, until a few hours ago, Claire hadn't even *liked* babies. Now she was taking it upon herself to see to one's needs, without panicking, and without having to be bribed. Nick didn't care what his inner voice was telling him. This was a good sign, dammit. And, by God, he was going to take it.

Step by step, he told himself. Little by little. Day by day. Maybe the long-term future was still pretty fuzzy, he conceded. But the short-term one was looking brighter all the time.

With a smile at the whisper of happiness and hopefulness that was humming in his veins, Nick pushed back the covers and rose to get dressed, too.

True to the good word of The Weather Channel, the snow did cease and desist for the rest of the day. The sun came out, hanging high in the sky like a bright promise, and it slowly melted a good bit of the snow that clung to the bushes and windows and eaves. The ground, however, was still blanketed with white, and the streets, though growing a bit slushy, were still mostly impassable. By nightfall, they were freezing up again.

Claire and Nick passed most of the day in a surprisingly peaceful fashion. Somehow, by mutual consensus, they were able to put on hold—for the time being—what had happened between them that morning. While Haley was awake, they played with her and fed her and cared for her, making idle chitchat about their lives these days, reminiscing over the safe, generic topics of their past. During the baby's afternoon nap, Nick made himself scarce by attacking the telephone again, trying to find someone who would know what to do about Haley's safekeeping.

Now, as night fell, Claire sat in her office with Haley in her lap, feeding the baby an after-dinner bottle of formula—with only the merest stains of blueberries and squash decorating her shirt and hair. And she watched Nick as he cradled a phone between shoulder and ear, and grew increasingly more agitated with whomever was on the other end of the line.

"I know there's nothing you can do to speed things along right now," he was saying. "I know it's nighttime, and Sunday to boot. But it's been almost twenty-four hours since this baby showed up here, and the trail isn't getting any fresher, if you know what I'm sayin'."

A long pause ensued, wherein Claire heard the buzz of a female voice from the other end of the line. It continued for some time with what sounded like an overly lengthy explanation of some kind, and Nick's shoulders drew more taut with each passing moment.

"I know that," he finally interjected, his patience clearly stretched to the limit. "But—"

More female buzzing.

"Yeah, but—"

Another lengthy explanation.

"But what I'm trying to say is—"

More buzzing.

"But—"

More explanation.

Call her an alarmist, but Claire didn't think Nick was making too much headway.

She sighed with resignation and conceded the battle, even if Nick refused to do so himself. Obviously they were going to be taking care of Haley for another night, at least.

Another night, she repeated to herself. With Haley. And with Nick. Thinking back on the way they had turned to each other this morning, she had no idea what to plan on for the evening ahead. For now, Haley seemed to be wide-awake, and although infant care was still a brave, new world to Claire, she suspected there was some kind of lengthy nighttime ritual that went along with putting a baby to bed for the night. For the next few hours, at least, she and Nick should be so preoccupied with Haley that they wouldn't have time to address the new developments that had come up between them.

However, once the baby was asleep, and they had a long, dark night stretching ahead of them…

Well, she decided, it was probably best not to worry about that right now. Yes, she and Nick would have to confront what had happened. And yes, they would have to decide where they were going to go from there. And yes, there was doubtless a rocky, unpredictable road they were would have to travel. But right now wasn't the time to start that particular journey.

A dry, sucking, slurpy sound brought her attention back
to the baby, even as Nick's argument with the faceless
woman on the phone escalated to new heights. Remembering how Haley had reacted earlier to the increased tension
between her and Nick, Claire decided it would probably be
better to take her into another room until he had finished
his conversation here.

So, hefting the plump little baby up onto her shoulder,
Claire palmed the empty bottle and headed back for the
kitchen. With one hand cupped over Haley's bottom, she
rinsed out the bottle and settled it into the dishwasher rack,
along with the remaining dishes from the dinner she and
Nick had shared. And, using just one hand, she stowed the
few leftovers in the big refrigerator.

She tried not to think about how it really wasn't all that
hard to adapt to life one-handed, when one was using the
other to cradle a baby who was singing in one's ear. And
she tried not to think about how very nice it had been to
share a meal in her home with another person for a change.

Usually, Claire either ate out on her way home from
work, or she picked something up on the way and consumed it in the study while she watched the evening news.
She seldom cooked, simply because she didn't much enjoy
the activity, and it seemed especially pointless when she
would only be doing it for one.

Thinking back now, in all the time she'd lived here, she
couldn't remember a single occasion when she'd shared her
kitchen table with another person. And somehow, the fact
that Nick had been the first to join her there just seemed
so oddly, utterly appropriate. She smiled wryly. She didn't
even usually make use of her dishwasher, because she gen-
erally dirtied too few dishes to bother. The stove, too, was
pretty much an alien appliance. The microwave was, after
all, the single person's best friend.

How strange that she had lived in this big house all this time and never entertained, she thought. And as long as she was thinking along those lines, how strange that she had bought this big house in the first place, when she'd had every intention of living here alone. It only now occurred to her how quiet and lonely the place had always been before. Before Haley's arrival on her doorstep. Before Nick had been blown in by the storm. But now, in less than twenty-four hours, the whole house felt different. Warmer. Cozier. Homier.

There was life here now, she realized. There was sound and motion. There was passion. There was love. There was everything necessary to generate a familylike existence. And for that reason, her house now felt like…well, it felt like a home.

Which meant that once Nick found out what to do with Haley, once he bundled her back up and took her off to wherever Social Services placed abandoned infants, then Claire's new home would revert to being just a house.

Just a house. And she would go back to living just a life.

"Looks like that's just the way it's going to be."

Nick's voice jarred her from her morose thoughts, and she forced a smile as she spun around to look at him. He sauntered into the kitchen looking tired and irritated, but the moment he glanced up to see her standing there with Haley, the clouds obscuring his expression lifted, and he smiled back.

"Thanks for cleaning up," he said.

She shrugged. "No problem."

"And thanks for cooking dinner."

Actually, Claire had microwaved dinner, but that was just a minor technicality. "No problem," she said again. "Really."

He sighed heavily. "Guess we're all going to be stuck together for another night. If that's okay with you?"

Unable to help herself, she asked, "And if it's not okay with me?"

He looked worried for a moment, then eyed her warily. "The snow's melted enough that I could probably make it back to my place tonight. It wouldn't be easy—or safe—but if you don't want me here, I can manage it."

Claire didn't hesitate. "I want you here."

He nodded, his relief evident, and she could scarcely believe he would have thought otherwise.

"Nick, I—"

"Claire, I—"

They both began talking at once, and both halted at once, then they began to chuckle nervously.

"You first," she said.

He shook his head. "You first."

She opened her mouth to say what she had begun to say, then realized she really didn't know what that was. Fortunately—or perhaps, unfortunately—Haley chose that moment to grab a fistful of her hair, then she gave it a swift tug. Hard.

"Ow!" Claire cried, reaching up to untangle the baby's fingers. Haley, however, decided this must be some kind of fun, wonderful game, because she yanked again, this time freeing completely the hair Claire had caught atop her head.

Nick laughed, then strode forward to give her a hand. After unwinding Haley's fingers from her hair, he lifted the baby from her arms and settled her into his instead. Claire took a moment to try and untangle a few of the sticky knots, then paused when she felt Nick's fingers glide through her hair, too.

"You have the most beautiful hair," he said softly. "You always did. I wish you hadn't cut it."

She tried to ignore the ripple of heat and euphoria that dappled her insides, and replied as coolly as she could—which really wasn't very cool at all—"It's easier to take care of this way. I don't have a lot of time to spend fixing it in the morning. This way, I can just blow it dry. Besides," she added, "it's not that short. It's still almost to my shoulders."

He nodded, but didn't release her hair. Instead, he ran his fingers through the straight tresses again. He probably wouldn't have stopped at all, except that Haley reached up for his nose again, giving it a playful honk.

"Hey, you," Nick said, chuckling. "Upset because you're suddenly not the center of the universe?"

The baby cooed long and low, then drooled on Nick's sweatshirt.

"Yeah, yeah. Guess I deserved that," he said.

When Claire focused on the baby again, she remembered what had occurred to her that morning, about her potential link to Haley's mother. She smacked her forehead soundly. "I can't believe I forgot. I meant to talk to you about this earlier," she said, "but with everything else going on, I just now remembered."

Everything else being, Claire thought, the fact that they had made such wild, uninhibited monkey love that morning, which probably wasn't such a good topic to bring up in any detail at the moment.

"What is it?" Nick asked. But she could see by the simmer of heat in his dark eyes that he was thinking exactly the same thing she was thinking about—namely, *everything else.*

With a deep, fortifying breath, Claire tried to ignore the way his heat was compounding her own and pressed on.

"What if Haley's mother was a patient of mine? Or a patient of one of the other doctors in my practice? There are five of us, and we have scores of patients. I didn't get a good enough look at the girl to see if she seemed at all familiar. But maybe that's why she singled me out?"

Nick nodded, rubbing a hand thoughtfully over his rough jaw. "That's a good point," he said. "And certainly possible. It's something I should have figured out myself." He didn't need to point out that he probably would have, too, if he hadn't been so preoccupied by…*everything else.* "Is there any way to check it out?"

"Not right this minute," she told him. "But tomorrow I can put the wheels in motion, provided some of the staff make it in through the snow. I'm supposed to go to work myself, so provided *I* can make it in, I'll start the search myself."

"I'll make sure you get in," he said. "I'll drive you myself."

"You don't have to do th—"

"I want to, Claire." His eyes fairly smoldered now as he added, "After all, I'll still be here in the morning, anyway."

Oh, fine, *just bring* that *up, why don't you?*

Fortunately, before that thought overwhelmed her completely, another one unfolded in her brain. There was actually an even more likely possibility that might link Haley's mother to Claire, and she couldn't imagine why it hadn't occurred to her before now. Probably because of *everything else* that had been going on.

"Oh, wait," she said softly, tentatively. "I think I know what it is. I bet I know what the connection is."

That, if nothing else, seemed to pull Nick's thoughts back to where they needed to be right now. "What?" he asked. "What's the connection?"

She didn't know why this hadn't occurred to her before. "I volunteer twice a month at a local women's clinic," she told him. "Every other week I teach a class for a couple of hours after school, helping pregnant teenagers take better care of themselves while they're pregnant. We talk about getting the proper nutrition, how it's essential to avoid drugs, cigarettes, alcohol, how they should try to get the baby's father involved if they can, that kind of thing.

"Nick!" she cried, convinced now that that was the link. It was the only one that made any sense. "I can't believe I didn't think about this right off. That's got to be it."

He gazed at her for a moment without speaking, as if he wanted to turn this new development over in his head a few times before commenting. Then, gradually, he began to nod. "How many girls do you see at a time?"

"It's a classroom environment," she told him, "but it's not really very structured. The girls come because they *want* to, not because anyone makes them. There could be anywhere from a half-dozen to two dozen in there at a time. And, as I said, it's only twice a month. A lot of the girls who start coming don't necessarily keep coming. Then again," she added thoughtfully, "a lot of them do. Some of them stay in the program right up through the birth of their child."

He nodded again. "It's a good start," he said. "You may be right. We'll definitely try that route, too."

The only problem was, Claire thought, it had been several months since Haley's mother would have been in the group—if, in fact, she had ever attended. And had she attended, she may have only come a handful of times. The clinic didn't keep accurate records for the class, because it was something Claire had instigated and organized and maintained herself. And she'd learned quickly that the best way to keep the girls coming was to ask as few questions as possible about their personal situations. She often didn't even know their last names, or even if the first names they gave her were real.

To Claire, of primary importance was the girls' health, because that, in turn, affected their babies' health. She hadn't cared what had brought them into the program in the first place, only that they got all the right information once they were there. And she wanted to encourage them to *use* the right information, because many of them received no encouragement at all elsewhere in their lives. Still, ultimately, it was always up to them to decide whether or not they *would* use it.

Although nothing frustrated Claire more than seeing girls or women who refused to take care of themselves when they were pregnant, she wasn't so naive that she thought she could change all their minds. In the long run, it was up to each woman as an individual to tend to herself and her child. It was just too bad that, sometimes, the babies paid the price for that.

"I'll have someone check the clinic tomorrow," Nick told her. "And, just to be on the safe side, you can have someone at your office start digging around there, too. Hopefully, one or the other will pan out."

"And if it doesn't?" she asked.

He shrugged. "Then I guess we're right back where we started from."

Funny, Claire thought. Ever since she'd opened her front door to find Nick Campisano standing on the other side, she'd been thinking exactly the same thing.

Nine

Nick stood in the doorway of the bathroom linked to Claire's bedroom, watching her as she bathed Haley, and unwilling to interrupt the two because they both seemed to be having so much fun. It hadn't been easy adapting the house to a baby who'd come with so few accessories, but they had managed. Right now, Haley was seated in a plastic laundry basket whose bottom half was opaque, and Claire was using a plastic cup full of water to rinse her. Fortunately, Claire was a profound proponent of Ivory soap, so finding a gentle cleanser hadn't been a problem. Haley's bath toys consisted of a funnel, a turkey baster, two spoons and a garlic press, and she was clearly ecstatic about each of them. She splashed and laughed and carried on with much delight as the water swirled around her.

Nick couldn't fight the laughter that rumbled up from deep inside him at her enthusiasm, and he released it in a burst of warm chuckles. "With all that joy she has for water, she's going to be an oceanographer someday," he said. "Mark my words."

Claire turned around so quickly at the sound of his voice that she lost her footing and sat down hard on the tiles. Her expression was etched with her obvious surprise at finding him there, but she only said, "Either that or a synchronized swimmer. There's more than a touch of Esther Williams in her."

As if wanting to punctuate that statement, Haley filled a tiny palm with water and hurled it at Claire's face. Then she laughed with glee as she watched the droplets dribble down Claire's cheeks.

"Correction," Claire said. "She's more like Esther Williams meets the Three Stooges."

Nick laughed harder, simply because at that moment, he just felt so damned good. There was something oddly comfortable and strangely right about the situation, something that generated a strong sense of peace and well-being inside him. It would be so easy to lie to himself right now, to tell himself that this was how things between him and Claire should have been. This was how it should be now. This was how it should be forever.

Unfortunately this would always be impossible for them unless they were both willing to make a few concessions.

"I think we're finished," Claire said.

For a moment, Nick felt a surge of panic rise up inside him, because, thanks to the course of his ruminations, he'd thought, for that moment, that she was talking about the two of them. Then he saw her lift the baby out of the water, holding Haley there while the last few dribbles of water dripped from the tiny, pudgy body. It seemed to be taking longer than necessary, however, because even when Haley began to squirm her irritation, Claire didn't let her go.

"Uh, Nick?" she asked.

"Yeah, Claire?"

"Um, what exactly is it that I'm supposed to do with her now?"

He smiled. "Well, it might sound unconventional, but, believe it or not, you're supposed to dry her off."

"Ah. I see. There, uh…there's just one problem with that, see."

"What is it?"

"I forgot to get a towel out for her."

He laughed again. "Yeah, that would be a problem, all right."

"Would you mind?" she asked. "There are some in the linen closet there beside you."

Naturally, a bathroom the size of the Taj Mahal would have a linen closet, Nick thought. He himself stowed his clean towels—all both of them—on a shelf over the toilet at his apartment. But when he opened the closet here, he found a vast, rainbow assortment of bath linens, enough to keep a small army dry and toasty.

Gee, Claire sure must take a lot of baths, he thought. Unless, of course, she was sharing these with someone else.…

Nah, definitely just a major cleannik, he decided, selecting a fat, fluffy towel from the top of the tallest stack. He was confident there was no one standing between him and Claire. Well, no one other than him and Claire, anyway.

He unfolded the towel, then held it open in silent invitation for her to pass the baby over to him. She smiled gratefully as she did just that, and Nick wrapped Haley up and carried her into the bedroom. He set her on the bed so that he could dry her off properly, then turned to Claire, who was watching them both with a dreamy look on her face that made Nick's heart hum with contentment. Haley was oblivious to them both, however, too intent on trying to get her toes into her mouth.

"You can do the diaper and jammies this time," Nick said impulsively.

Claire's smile faltered "But I—"

"Hey," he interrupted her, "you have yet to change one single diaper on this kid. I've done every last one."

She gaped at him in disbelief. "Well, I've fed her every time."

"That's 'cause you're a sucker," he told her with a smile.

She stuck her tongue out at him in return. "Yeah, and I'm not going to get suckered into this," she pointed out.

"Claire, Claire, Claire," he said patiently, shaking his head slowly as he feigned a serious, father-knows-best tone. "Now I know you're a busy woman and everything, but I don't see why you shouldn't share in some of the responsibilities here. Haley is your daughter, too, ya know. And I think it's time you started pulling your half of the parental weight around here."

Nick had meant for the comment to be a joke, but Claire evidently didn't take it that way at all. "Haley is *not* my daughter," she countered, looking almost stricken for some reason. "And she is *not* my responsibility. Don't you dare suggest otherwise."

Ooo, *way* touchy, Nick thought. And he couldn't quite decide if that was good or bad. Ultimately he decided not to ponder it at all. Not for the time being, at any rate. After all, they had far too many other things to address right now. Like, for instance, tonight's sleeping arrangements.

"I'll go downstairs and fix up a bottle," he said. "You can diaper and change her."

"But—"

"Do it, Claire," he instructed her in his best, no-

nonsense voice. "It's your turn to change her, my turn to feed her. We might as well get used to both roles, because, hey, let's face it, we might just be doing this for another day and night. Or more."

Leaving her to make what she would of that comment, Nick left her alone with Haley, knowing that with every additional moment she spent with the baby, Claire grew a bit more comfortable and a bit less hesitant with the whole baby thing. With any luck at all, he thought as he headed for the kitchen, one more night—and perhaps one more morning—would afford her enough exposure to infants to at least make her reevaluate her opinion of them.

Nick didn't dare hope that she might completely come around to his way of thinking. He didn't dare hope that she might someday consent to having a half-dozen kids of her own. But maybe, just maybe, she'd agree to three or four. Hey, it could happen.

"Compromise," he murmured to himself as he entered her kitchen to prepare a bottle for Haley. "That's the word of the day. All we have to do is figure out a way to compromise."

Claire disappeared while Nick was giving Haley her final bottle and rocking her to sleep, so once he had the baby down for the night, he retreated for a little while, too. Hey, she couldn't go far, he reasoned, and maybe she needed her space for a bit, to figure out—as he was hoping to do—just what she wanted from the night ahead.

He showered and shaved—okay, so maybe *he* already knew what he wanted from the night ahead; so sue him—then retired to the room where he had passed the previous night. He donned a pair of exhausted sweatpants and a faded, stretched-out T-shirt that read Vinnie's House Of Hubcaps, then lay down barefoot on the bed with a copy of *The Atlantic Monthly* that he'd found downstairs. In the study. On top of the console. Right next to the wine rack.

Oh, and he'd also opened what promised to be a very nice pinot noir, and he'd left the open bottle on the dresser—along with two glasses—to let it breathe a bit before he'd pour it.

All in all, he decided, life was pretty damned good. At least, for the moment.

When he'd come back upstairs with the wine, he'd heard the water running in the hallway bathroom, and had decided that, unless Haley had just taken a giant developmental leap forward, then Claire was readying herself for bed, too. As he lay in bed now, he was playing a kind of mental roulette with himself, trying to figure out which bedroom Claire would return to once she'd finished with her evening ablutions. And if she chose her room over his, then what was he going to do about it?

Make her change her mind, he decided. That's what he was going to do about it. And he'd use whatever weapons he had at his disposal to win her over.

As luck—and hopefully a few other things—would have it, however, that didn't appear as if it would be necessary. Because just as Nick finished pouring two glasses of wine, he heard a soft whisper of sound at his bedroom door, and turned to find Claire standing framed there.

She looked incredible, he thought, dressed in a long silky gown the color of pale gold champagne, with a robe of the same soft fabric opening over it. The hems of both garments swept the floor above satin slippers, and where the bottom half of the gown was shimmeringly smooth, the top half was sheer lace, through which he could see the dusky valley between her breasts. Once she removed the robe, he thought, he'd also be able to see the dark circles of her—

Best not to think about that just yet, he told himself. No

need to rush. They had plenty of time. All night, in fact. And he didn't intend to waste a moment of it.

It didn't escape him that her ensemble was the kind of thing a woman might choose to wear on her wedding night. Then he forced himself to stop thinking along those lines, too, because it was a very dangerous route to take.

"Hi," he said as calmly as he could, hoping she could detect neither the raging of his heartbeat, nor the thunder of his desire. "Wine?" he asked.

Whoa, way to go, Campisano, he thought, squeezing his eyes shut at how dim-witted he sounded. *Conversation 101 is a total success. I think you're ready to move into multisyllable statements now.*

"Yes, thank you," she said, taking a few steps toward him. "Wine sounds very good."

"I, uh…I was kinda worried you wouldn't come," he told her quietly but unabashedly as he handed her a glass.

She expelled an anxious sound. "That's funny. I was worried that I wouldn't be able to stay away. Looks like my worries were well-founded, weren't they?" Her eyes grew sad for some reason as she added, "Because I just can't seem to stay away from you."

"Why would you want to?" he asked. "Why would that worry you?"

She met his gaze levelly as she cupped the bowl of her wineglass with a nervous grip. "Because I'm still not sure what's going on between us, Nick," she said softly. "I still don't know what the future holds for us. I still don't know how we're going to be able to work things out. And if they don't work out, I don't know how I'm going to be able to walk away from you a second time."

His heart hummed happily behind his rib cage, even though he couldn't offer her any clear-cut answers for her concern. So all he told her was, "Just don't think about that right now."

She gaped at him. "Are you kidding? I can't think about anything else."

"Then maybe I need to distract you."

Her eyes widened at that, and she lifted her glass to her lips for a generous taste of wine. Nick mimicked the action himself, savoring the mellow smoky flavor before swallowing. However, the splash of heat that warmed his belly did nothing to soothe the tremor of anticipation that shook the rest of him.

"I, uh…I feel a little underdressed," he said impulsively, striving for a lightness he was nowhere close to feeling, wondering how miserably he failed in his effort.

"*You* feel underdressed," Claire replied with a nervous chuckle, pushing her robe closed over her midsection. "I've never worn this before, even though I bought it years ago. I had no idea it was so… I mean… I don't even know why I bought it in the first place. It's so…"

Hastily she ceased talking, as if she feared overstating what she'd already made clear. At least, it was clear to Nick. She sipped her wine again, then clutched the robe more tightly over herself.

"Don't," he said, reaching out to undo her gesture. When he tugged the robe open again, he overcompensated, and it fell open to clearly reveal one of her breasts. Instinctively Claire lifted a hand to conceal herself again, but Nick beat her to it, confidently cupping his hand over the warm, lace-covered mound.

"Don't hide yourself, not for me," he said, closing his fingers gently over her. He smiled at the sigh of delight that feathered over her lips with the contact. "You look so…" He couldn't quite stop the sigh that escaped him, as well. "You look so beautiful, Claire. You look like…"

"Like what?" she asked.

"Like a bride," he told her.

She bit her lip at his suggestion, but said nothing to deny or confirm that she'd been striving for just that image. No longer interested in calming himself or her with the wine, Nick set his glass on the dresser and then reached for Claire's. She relinquished it without objection, her gaze never leaving his, then stepped forward to close what little distance was left between them.

And then, just as he had helped himself to possession of her, Claire reached for Nick. She cupped her hand over that most masculine part of him, then slowly, methodically, stroked him from head to base.

"Oh," he murmured. "Oh, Claire."

She grinned triumphantly at his easy acquiescence and her total command, then raked her fingertips along his lusty length again. Up and down she journeyed over the fabric along his shaft, rubbing her palm leisurely over the head. He stiffened and ripened as she held him, growing more plump and demanding with every motion. Finally, Claire dipped her hand inside the waistband of his sweats and wrapped her fingers firmly around his hot, ample flesh.

A blast of fire shot through Nick at the feel of her skin against his, and he knew that their initial joining tonight would be much faster and more demanding than it had been that morning. As Claire continued to stroke him, he dropped his hands to her hips and bunched her gown in both fists. Up, up, up he pulled the fabric, over her legs and thighs and taut derriere. As he'd hoped, she wore nothing beneath, and he splayed both hands open over her warm, smooth, naked bottom.

Her hand faltered on him momentarily at the contact, but she recovered admirably, pulling her hand slowly over him again. So Nick intensified his attentions in an effort to slow

her down. He dipped the fingers of both hands into the
elegant cleft bisecting her fanny, pulling, pushing, probing
his way gradually down to the moist folds of flesh between
her legs. Without being asked, Claire shuffled one foot to
the side, opening herself to him completely.

Immediately he took advantage of her silent offer, sliding
a long finger against and inside her, over and over and over
again.

"Oh," Claire murmured this time. "Oh, Nick..."

The catch in her voice when she spoke his name was
ultimately his undoing. Not wanting to be separated from
her for even an instant longer, he urged her body backward,
toward the bed. When she stood between him and it, Nick
gently nudged her backward, until she lay across the mattress with her feet still on the floor, and her gown bunched
up around her waist. With her ebony hair spread around
her head, with her arms arced gracefully above her, with
her full breasts straining against the transparent lace of her
gown, she looked like a painting of a wanton—and extremely erotic—temptation.

Nick folded his body into hers, opening his mouth over
the lace that covered one dark nipple. Again and again he
laved her with the flat of his tongue, sucking both fabric
and flesh deep into his mouth. Through a foggy haze of
euphoria, he felt her insistent fingers tangle in his hair, felt
her slender body buck against his belly. And he realized he
simply could not stand it anymore. Standing, without un-
dressing, he shoved down his sweats and entered her
deeply, thrusting harder with every forceful movement of
her body against his. Claire wrapped her legs around his
waist to pull him deeper still, and Nick strove to accom-
modate her every demand.

He couldn't seem to get enough of her, knew deep down
he would never, ever, have enough of her. Yet, still he

struggled to possess her completely. And still he fought to give all of himself to her.

He felt the shudder of completion override him with the force of an earthquake, and it seemed like the passage of an eternity before he finally spilled himself into her. Even after he was empty, for long moments he continued to propel his body forward into hers. Claire, too, appeared to be unwilling to release him. Somehow he feared that in removing himself from inside her, he would lose a part of himself forever. And somehow he sensed that she felt the same way.

Ultimately, however, he did withdraw from her, but only physically, and only long enough to remove his clothes and join her on the bed. He kissed her deeply, insistently, resolutely, as he lay down beside her, and she roped her arms around his neck to return his embrace with equal fire. Somehow they freed her gown from the rest of her body and discarded it onto the floor. And then they clung to each other, skin to skin, heart to heart, their bodies slick with passion and perspiration, holding on as if each were terrified of ever letting go.

''Never leave me,'' Nick said softly as he tucked his head into the curve of her chin and shoulder. His damp breath beaded her nipple and, still unable to keep from touching her, he caressed the tight bud with the pad of his thumb. ''Promise me, Claire,'' he said softly. ''Never leave me.''

But through the haze and glow of loving aftermath, all he heard was a sigh of contentment and the rapid pounding of her heart. It was only as sleep overcame him that Nick realized she had never answered him at all.

The telephone ringing jarred Claire awake the following morning, rousing her from a dream in which she and Nick were sitting together at her kitchen table, sharing coffee over the morning paper. It was the most boring dream she'd ever had. And the most wonderful.

She started to fumble for her telephone, then realized there was a warm, solid, very male body between her and it. That body, too, seemed to be on the move—however slowly—and appeared to be reaching for the receiver on the nightstand beside him.

Still clearly half-asleep, Nick fumbled the phone against his ear and mumbled, "'Lo?"

Claire couldn't help the smile that curled her lips. She found herself halfway hoping that there was someone on the other end of the line who knew her well—or, at least, who *thought* they knew her well—someone who would be pumping her for information about the rugged, rough, rusty male voice that had greeted them from her phone at— She squinted through the semidarkness at the glowing blue numerals on her clock. At 6:45 in the morning. Rather incriminating evidence, that.

And rather delightful.

What a night, she thought, feeling lusty and lethargic and content. She and Nick had slept for a few hours after that first union, only to be awakened by Haley's soft cries just before two o'clock. Claire had donned her robe and had sleepily prepared a bottle, then had brought the baby into Nick's room to feed her. As she'd leaned against the headboard holding Haley, Nick had sat up to watch them. The sheet had dipped low around his waist, and his naked torso had appeared painted with silver in the semidarkness.

When Haley had finished, Claire had returned her to her bedroom to rock her back to sleep. Then she herself had returned to Nick's bed, where they'd repeated—more slowly and thoroughly this time—the heated union of their bodies.

And now it was morning, she thought, and with daybreak came a host of considerations that the darkness of night had readily obscured. Not the least of which, she thought further, was the phone call that had roused them.

Nick was silent for a second after his initial half greeting, then, with some difficulty, he managed to identify himself. Sort of. "Yeah. This…Dec'tif…uh, Dective…uh… This is Campisano."

Claire had begun to snuggle quite comfortably into his heat and strength when his entire body suddenly went rigid beneath her. Slowly he sat up, bringing her with him, then circled his arm automatically around her shoulders. She tugged the sheet and blanket up to her neck to ward off the morning chill, but Nick let it slump unheeded to his waist.

"You don't say," he said into the phone.

In response, someone did say. Something. Claire just couldn't hear what.

"Yeah, definitely," he returned.

That was followed by a couple of *Uh-huhs,* which were, in turn, followed by three *Nuh-uhs.* And then one more *Uh-huh.*

"No, I don't think that will be a problem at all," he finally said, speaking English once again like a pro. "Just give us a couple of hours to get things squared away here. I'm not sure how the roads are, but—"

More buzzing from the other end, but Claire thought she deciphered the word, "Snowplows."

"Oh, yeah?" Nick said, his voice bland in response to such good news. "Well, that's just great." Funny, but he didn't sound like he thought it was great. "Then it shouldn't be a problem at all. No, we'll be there as soon as we can. And thanks."

Without offering a goodbye, Nick dropped the telephone receiver back into the cradle, then stared off into space.

"Nick?" Claire said. "What is it? What's wrong?"

For a minute, she didn't think he'd heard her, because he only continued to gaze blindly at the wall on the other side of the room. She was about to give his arm a good shake, when he finally turned to look at her.

"That was someone down at the station, returning one of the calls I made yesterday," he said.

A hot wave of discontent washed along Claire's belly. "And?" she asked.

Nick met her gaze levelly. "They found Haley's mother."

Ten

The first thing Claire noticed about Haley's mother, without having the hindrances of darkness and snowfall and flawed glass to obscure her features, was that, along with her long, blond hair, the young woman had a big black eye. The second thing Claire noticed about her was that she had a puffy, split lip. The third thing she noticed was that she appeared to be even younger than Claire had initially thought. And the next thing she noticed was that the girl was clearly terrified.

Sixteen years old, Claire guessed. Certainly not much more than that. And she'd obviously had a rough time of it. In addition to being beaten up, the girl was skinny and pale and frail looking. Either she didn't get enough to eat, or she had a drug habit or eating disorder of some kind. Her clothing would have hung better on a scarecrow. The black leather jacket looked like it must belong to a man

three times her size, and her black jeans were baggy around
the hips.

A woman with a young baby should still be carrying
some excess weight, Claire thought. She should be rounded
and filled out and well fed. Certainly she shouldn't look
like a half-starved refugee. But she suspected that, in many
ways, that was precisely what Haley's mother was.

"My baby?" the girl said the moment she looked up and
saw Claire and Nick enter the room.

When she leapt up from her chair and approached them,
Nick immediately stepped between her and Claire, who
held Haley against her shoulder with one of the baby's pink
blankets tented over her head. Haley had drooled a bit on
Claire's ivory sweater, and Claire still carried a few applesauce stains from breakfast on her blue jeans, but all in all,
she and the baby complemented each other perfectly. Claire
tried her best not to think just how perfectly.

The girl halted at Nick's intercession, her maternal instincts obviously warring with her survival instincts—and
very nearly winning. Nick wore what he had been wearing
the night he'd shown up at Claire's front door—My God,
she thought, had it only been two nights ago?—and did
look more than a little intimidating in his oversize sweater,
blue jeans, enormous hiking boots and big Nanook of the
North parka. But even though Haley's mother hesitated, she
angled her body to gaze around him, at Claire and the baby.

"Is that my baby?" she asked earnestly, the note of des-
peration in her voice nearly breaking Claire's heart. "Is that
Haley? Is she okay? Please tell me she's okay."

"She's fine," Claire assured her.

Nick swung around to glare at her, obviously not wanting
to impart any more information about Haley than was absolutely essential.

"Well, she *is* fine," Claire retorted to his silent, but unmistakable anger. Ignoring it, she turned to Haley's mother again. "Everything's okay," she said. "Your baby is perfectly all right. Here," she added impulsively as she drew Haley away from her shoulder, "see for yourself."

It was all the invitation the girl needed. Even the imposing, thunderous presence of Dominic Campisano couldn't deter her then. She took a few more steps forward, made a *wi...i...ide* arc around Nick—whom she likewise eyed with *much* caution—and came up alongside Claire. The moment she did, Haley began to coo and wiggle with clear delight and reached out with much rejoicing for her mommy.

Claire decided not to ponder for the moment the fact that the baby didn't appear to be at all frightened by her mother's state of being battered, something which could only indicate that this wasn't the first time Haley had seen her that way. A wave of melancholy unrolled in Claire's stomach, but for now she focused on the happier aspects of the reunion.

"Oh, sweetie," the girl said. "Oh, Haley. Mommy missed you *so much*. Mommy loves you *so much*."

She snuggled the baby against her breasts in a manner that showed quite clearly it was a gesture she performed often. Then she curled her entire body over Haley's as if by doing so, she might somehow protect the child from imminent—or any other—harm. Then she began to sway her body back and forth, crooning soft, incoherent words of love that the baby returned with quiet enthusiasm. Even when Haley filled both little fists full of blond hair and yanked hard—the pain of which Claire remembered, too well, could bring tears to her eyes—the girl's only reaction was to laugh happily.

"Oh, Haley..." she said, sniffling, crowding the infant's body even closer to her own. "Oh, my baby..."

And then Claire realized that the baby's mother wasn't

the only one who was crying. She was becoming a little weepy herself.

"Vivian, we still have a lot of work ahead of us," a new voice interjected.

Claire's attention—along with Nick's and the baby's and the girl's—turned to the woman still seated at the desk where Haley's mother had been sitting when they first arrived. She looked to be in her mid- to late fifties, was of slender build, with salt-and-pepper hair, dark, wide-spaced eyes, and skin the color of rich coffee.

"I'm Annette Graham," she said. "I'm with Social Services." She stood and approached Nick. "You must be Detective Campisano. We spoke on the phone."

Nick nodded as he extended his hand to the other woman. "Nick is fine," he said. "Thanks for contacting me, Ms. Graham," he said.

She gave his hand a couple of vigorous shakes and replied, "Thanks for staying on top of this. And please, call me Annette." She tilted her head toward Haley and her mother, who were so intent on getting reacquainted that they didn't seem to notice anyone else at all. "This is Vivian Dixon," she continued. "She's told us quite a tale since last night, but it's one we've been able to validate pretty well. Unfortunately."

She ran down the specifics quickly and dispassionately, and as Claire listened, she grew more and more morose. Before becoming pregnant with Haley, Vivian Dixon had spent a good five months on the streets of Philadelphia. Before that, she had lived in a small town in the Maryland panhandle, where she had grown up.

Although "lived," Claire decided, was a deceptive term. According to Annette, Vivian's mother was an alcoholic, and her father had abandoned them both when Vivian was just a baby. By the time the girl entered high school, she was pretty much relying on herself for survival—and dodging the unwanted attentions of her mother's latest boyfriend.

She'd run away from home the day after her sixteenth birthday and was now seventeen. She'd become pregnant by a twenty-nine-year-old South Jersey bartender whose sole purpose in life seemed to be to control her every move, and to own every aspect of her person. At first, Vivian had thought his overpowering intrusion into her life—into her soul—had been a result of his consuming love for her. Ultimately, however, she'd learned the hard way that what he felt for her wasn't love at all.

"He never hurt the baby, though," Vivian interrupted when Annette Graham got to this part of the story. "I always made sure Haley was out of the way whenever Donnie was...um...in one of his moods. And Donnie never raised a hand to her."

Only then did Claire remember that Vivian had been listening to the details of her life unfold before two strangers, without comment or embellishment, neither disagreeing with what was said, nor offering any clarification for any of it. Claire supposed that a girl who had experienced a life like hers became matter-of-fact about things pretty quickly.

Nick and Annette also seemed surprised when the girl finally spoke up, as if they, too, had forgotten she was even in the room.

"He didn't," Vivian insisted, seeming determined to defend a man who had beaten her black-and-blue. She must have understood immediately that she appeared to be doing just that, because her expression twisted a bit and she began to backpedal. "I'm not defending him. Really, I'm not. Not anymore. What he did..." She hesitated, then glanced back down at Haley, obscuring her face and expression.

"Well, he shouldn't have done it, that's all," she went

on quietly. "And Saturday, when it happened again..." Once more her voice trailed off, and once more she rallied herself to continue. "I started thinking that if he did it to me, he could do it to Haley, too. And I just couldn't let that happen to her. I couldn't let him—or anybody—hurt her. But I couldn't defend her by myself. Donnie is just so...he's so... I mean...he's not the kind of guy you mess with, you know?"

"Yeah, he's the kind of guy who beats up young girls who are a quarter of his size, isn't he?"

The barely restrained fury in Nick's voice was matched only by the barely restrained fury in his body. Claire knew him well enough to know that had the nefarious Donnie been present in the room at that moment he wouldn't have had much longer to live.

Normally, Claire deplored even the merest suggestion of violence. Normally, there was absolutely no reason for one person to lift a hand to another. Normally, she viewed any hostile intentions as primitive, immature and dangerous. That said, however, there were some people in the world— like this Donnie, for instance—whom Claire would very much like to see get the stuffing beaten out of them. Preferably more than once.

Vivian nodded at Nick's statement, but said nothing more in comment. She did look back up at them again when she added, "I knew I needed to leave him, but I didn't have anyplace else to go. I didn't have anyplace to take Haley. Donnie's been everything to me since I met him. I don't have any friends that weren't his friends first, and they would have told him where I was in a heartbeat. I couldn't go back home, and I just...I just..."

Tears filled her eyes again, tumbling down her face even as she tipped her head backward in an effort pull them back in. "I just...I didn't have anywhere to take her," she said again. "But I couldn't stay there with him anymore, because he might have hurt her. I can take care of myself on the streets," she added with forced valiance, appearing all the more pathetic for her effort. "I did it for a long time before I met Donnie. But I couldn't take care of Haley there. It wouldn't have been safe for her. No place was safe for her."

"What about shelters?" Claire asked. "There are some very good shelters for women in your situation. Why didn't you try one of those?"

A shadow crossed Vivian's face at the suggestion. "I was afraid they'd take Haley away from me. I was afraid they'd look at me, and they'd know I couldn't take care of her, and they'd put her in foster care. I've been in foster care before," she added somberly. "And I didn't want that for Haley. I wanted her to have a good life with somebody who would want her. Who would love her. Who would make sure she was happy."

"But why me?" Claire asked. "I'm a total stranger to you. What made you think that I would want or love or be able to take care of your baby?"

For a moment, Vivian didn't answer. She only nibbled her lip in thought as Haley threaded her fingers through the long shafts of blond that spilled over her shoulders. Finally she said, "You weren't a stranger. Not totally, anyway."

Claire nodded. "You were a patient at the women's clinic, weren't you?"

Vivian nodded silently.

"You came to some of the prenatal care classes I taught, right?"

Another silent nod.

"I'm sorry," Claire said. "But I don't remember you."

Vivian sighed. "I didn't come all the time. And when I did, I sat in the back. I'm not very comfortable in crowds.

And a lot of times…'' She shrugged philosophically. ''A lot of times, I didn't want anybody to see how I looked.''

''But you did come,'' Claire said.

''Yeah. And I always liked you. I thought you seemed really…I don't know. Nice. You seemed like you really cared about what you were doing. I started wondering if maybe the reason you did the classes at the clinic was because you didn't have kids of your own to take care of. I thought maybe that's why you decided to become the kind of doctor you did—because you liked babies so much. I thought maybe you couldn't have any of your own. Or maybe you hadn't found the right guy to be the father.'' She shrugged again, and there was an innocence about the gesture that touched Claire's heart. ''You just seemed really…I don't know…lonely and stuff. Like you didn't have a family to go home to, so you made the clinic your family instead.''

At Vivian's simply offered observation, all the air left Claire's lungs in a rapid *whoosh*. Her heart rate accelerated and her skin grew hot, and she told herself there couldn't possibly any truth in what the girl had said.

Could there?

No, surely not.

In spite of her background, she was just a naive kid in a lot of ways. She had assumed things about Claire with an adolescent's view of the world. She had drawn conclusions based on her ideals, not with any knowledge of Claire's situation. She didn't know Claire as a person at all. Claire knew herself better than anyone. There was no way what Vivian said could be right.

Could it?

No, surely not.

Vivian seemed not to notice Claire's reaction, though, because she continued on blithely, ''And you always seemed kind of sad to me. Like your life was kind of empty or something, and you needed somebody to be a part of it.''

Her life was *not* empty, Claire told herself. Her job kept her very busy, and she had her volunteer work. She had friends and she went out sometimes, and there was no way on earth her life could be empty, even if, over the last couple of days, that very thought had uncurled in her own head more than once. Vivian couldn't possibly be right.

Could she?

No, surely not.

''When I first started wondering about who might be able to take care of Haley,'' Vivian continued, ''who might really want her and be able to love her, I thought about everybody I'd met over the last year. And when my brain hit on you, I just couldn't budge it. Every time I tried to come up with someone else, I just kept thinking about you. I thought maybe Haley could keep you company. I thought maybe she could keep you from being lonely and sad. I thought maybe you'd like to have her in your life, that you'd be able to love her, because you didn't seem to have anyone else.

''But I can't give her up now,'' she hastened on, as if she feared Claire would indeed try to keep Haley. ''I can't stand the thought of never seeing her again. I got as far as the bus station Saturday night, and I realized there was no way I could leave her, even with you. But by then the snow was coming down way too hard, and I couldn't make it back to your house. And then I thought maybe it would be better to come here, to the police, instead. I was afraid you wouldn't give Haley back to me.''

Claire lifted a hand to cover her face, hoping nobody could detect the turmoil that was eating her up inside. She'd barely heard a word of Vivian's insistence that she wanted to keep her baby, because she was far too consumed by the first part of the girl's statement instead.

Had Claire been motivated all this time by some subconscious need for a family? *Had* she become an obstetrician because she'd had something other than a medical and scientific interest in babies and human reproduction? *Had* she instigated the clinic program because she wanted to have someone to take care of, seeing as how there was no one else in her life for whom she could perform that function?

Could it be possible that, all along, all this time, she had wanted the very things she had so steadfastly avoided? A husband, children, a happy, domestic home life? Had she simply wasted the last twelve years?

Immediately she knew that last wasn't true at all. She had always enjoyed her studies and her profession. There was no way she could consider her education and career wasted. But could she have somehow combined them with Nick during those years? Had the two of them been less stubborn, could they have survived marriage and children and everything else?

When she felt a large, warm hand cup the back of her neck, Claire realized that Nick knew exactly what was going through her head. And when she turned to look at him, she realized that it was because he, too, was thinking the same thing. Like Claire, he was wondering if the two of them had missed out on so much over the last dozen years because neither had been willing to compromise. Like Claire, he was reminding himself that, in the long run, they'd both ended up unhappy and unfulfilled anyway.

And, like Claire, he was wondering if there was any way on earth that the two of them might make up for lost time.

"Oh, Nick…" she said softly. But somehow she could think of nothing else to add.

He seemed to understand completely, though, because he looped an arm across her shoulders and pulled her close, then pressed a soft kiss to her temple. Aloud, all he said was, "What are we gonna do about all this?"

Vivian Dixon, however, seemed to think he was talking about something else, because, in a voice filled with panic, she said, "You can't take my baby from me. You just can't. I know I shouldn't have done what I did, but I didn't know what else to do. Do you understand me? *I didn't know what else to do!*"

"Vivian," Annette Graham said, cupping a motherly hand over the girl's shoulder. "Like I said, we have a lot of work to do. Don't jump to any conclusions right now. Best-case scenario, with some counseling and hard work, you and Haley will be fine."

Vivian eyed the woman warily. "And worst-case scenario?" she asked.

Annette's lips thinned in what even Claire could tell was her disapproval of the possibility. "Worst case, Haley will go into foster care."

Tears filled Vivian's eyes at the mere suggestion, and she made no effort to fight them. "No," she said, her voice breaking on the word. "That can't happen. You can't do that to her. You can't do that to me. Haley is all I have. I tried to do the right thing. I did. I'm sorry. I just…I didn't know what else to do."

"I know," Annette said, gripping the girl's shoulder more firmly. "And I promise you that I will do whatever is within my power to make sure you keep the baby. But Vivian, you have to understand that what you did in leaving Haley at Dr. Wainwright's was very, very serious. And you're going to have to make some massive changes in your life if you don't want to lose her."

"I'll do anything," she said eagerly. "Anything. What-

ever you tell me to do, I'll do it. Whatever it takes to make
sure I keep Haley, I'll do it. Just tell me what to do.
Please.''

Annette nodded. ''For now, you and your baby can just
sit in here and get reacquainted. I'd like to have a little chat
with Detective Campisano and Dr. Wainwright.''

She moved past Nick and Claire, and Claire was turning
around to follow her when Vivian's soft voice made her
hesitate.

''Dr. Wainwright? Thank you. For taking such good care
of Haley, I mean.''

Claire smiled, albeit a little sadly. ''She's a wonderful
little baby,'' she said. ''You've done remarkably well with
her.'' Especially considering the kind of life the girl had
been living since Haley's birth. But Claire didn't figure she
needed to point that out. ''Would it be okay if I held her
one more time?'' she asked, surprising herself enormously.

Vivian, however, seemed not to be surprised by the re-
quest at all. She just smiled and nodded. ''Sure.''

Claire saw Nick and Annette hesitate behind her, but she
didn't care. She took Haley from her mother and held her
close, stroking her curled index finger over the baby's
downy cheek. ''You're a sweet girl,'' she said softly. ''You
be good for your mommy.''

''Ooooo,'' Haley said. Then she smiled and lifted a
pudgy finger toward Claire's face, poking her in the nose
before opening her little, drool-stained hand flat over her
cheek.

Claire couldn't help but chuckle, nor could she quite
keep herself from brushing a soft kiss over the baby's forehead.

''She likes you,'' Vivian said as she took the baby back
into possession. ''You should have a few kids of your own,
you know. You'd be a good mom.''

"Truer words were never spoken," Nick said softly from behind her.

Claire decided not to respond to either comment. For now. Nor would she even think about the suggestion. For now. Her emotions were all in a jumble after the weekend and the morning she'd just spent. There was no way she could weed through them all to figure out what was what.

"Mrs. Graham?" Vivian called out as Claire made her way to join Nick and the social worker.

"Yes, Vivian?"

As she had when Claire and Nick had first arrived, the girl once again looked terrified. "What if… I mean, about Donnie…?"

"Yes?" Annette asked.

"What if he—what if he finds out where me and Haley are? What if he comes looking for us? I mean, I know he doesn't love us, but he…he wants us. If you know what I mean. I don't think he'll just disappear."

Claire was familiar enough with men like Donnie—through her studies and her patients, if not through personal experience—to know that Vivian had a valid fear on her hands. Evidently Annette realized that, too.

"I'll see what I can do about getting a protective order," the social worker said.

"I don't think that'll be necessary," Nick told her.

All three women turned to him in obvious surprise.

"Why not?" Claire asked. "He's obviously a dangerous man."

Nick pulled himself up to his full height and inhaled a deep, steadying breath. "You give me Donnie's address," he told Vivian. "I'll go pay him a little visit. I'll make it more than clear to him that if he *ever* tries to mess with Haley *or* you he'll have to come through me first. And I promise you, Vivian, if he does that—" Nick cracked his knuckles menacingly. "Well, let me put it this way. He *might* live to tell the tale, but he'll sure as hell wish he hadn't. Don't think I won't make that clear to him."

Across the hall from the room where they'd left Vivian and Haley in the company of another social worker, Nick and Claire sat down in folding chairs with Annette Graham to discuss the girl's future. Nick sat on one side of the table, Claire on the other, and the social worker perched herself at the head, forming a perfect triad. Somehow, Nick thought, they seemed to be circling the wagons, or fortifying the keep.

He had to confess that, when he had first been informed that Haley's mother had come forward, he'd been ready to do everything within his power to make sure the woman was never allowed near the child again. He'd been so certain that anyone who could abandon her own flesh and blood the way Vivian Dixon had, then that person had given up any and all rights to her child.

Now, however, having met Vivian and having seen what kind of person she was, having heard the kind of experiences she'd survived and having realized what had driven her to do what she'd done…

God, she was still just a kid herself, he thought. A kid who'd been beaten up—more than once—by some slimy sonofabitch three times her size who Nick personally couldn't wait to get his hands on. But despite everything that Vivian had been through, it was clear that she genuinely loved her baby. She honestly wanted what was best for Haley. She'd really had only the baby's best interests at heart when she'd left Haley on Claire's doorstep Saturday night. She'd just been too scared and panicked to think reasonably.

But she *had* left Haley on Claire's doorstep, he reminded

himself. And that was still a damned serious charge, regardless of her state of mind when she'd done it. And he wasn't going to let her off the hook easily.

"So what's the big picture here?" he asked Annette Graham, who, like so many social workers of Nick's acquaintance, seemed to really want the best outcome for the situation. She seemed to be behind Vivian one hundred percent, but she was obviously realistic and wary enough not to jump right in with the "Somewhere Over the Rainbow" speech.

"Big picture," she repeated. "Vivian is in a lot of trouble right now. The courts don't look favorably upon teenage mothers in general, and one who abandoned her baby—in a snowstorm, no less—doesn't offer up the most rousing image of maternal love.

"However," she added when she heard Nick's sigh of defeat, "there is some hope. Camden County recently introduced a program for teen mothers that's been getting some remarkably good results. I'd like to see about getting Vivian included in it. She's a good candidate. Until now, she's never been in trouble with the law. She's drug-free and in good health, all things considered, she's intelligent and eager to make the changes necessary to care for herself and her baby. I think we could probably get her admitted."

"What kind of program?" Claire asked, before Nick had the chance. She, too, was eager for a happy ending where Haley and Vivian were concerned.

"Vivian will have to go back to school and get her high school diploma," Annette said, "and she'll be required to work a part-time job ten hours a week. She'll attend additional classes about child care and parenting, and she'll also receive some vocational training. The state will provide day care for Haley during those times."

"Or I could," Claire piped up. When Nick and Annette

both glanced over at her in surprise, she hastened to clarify, "I—I mean…I'd be happy to watch Haley a couple of times a week myself. It, uh—it would be fun."

Nick smiled at the offer, thinking Claire was coming along really nicely with the whole kids thing. Maybe….

"The state will also give Vivian a stipend for living allowances," Annette went on, scattering his thoughts—for now—"provided she stays in the program and doesn't get into any more trouble. A social worker will visit her regularly and make sure she's seeing to the baby's needs.

"It sounds a lot easier than it is," she concluded, "but I think Vivian can do it. There's just one catch," she added, her voice flat.

"What's that?" Nick and Claire chorused as one.

"Vivian will have to have a sponsor who will be there to support her for the entirety of the program. And according to her, there's no one in her life that's willing to do something like that for her."

"What does this sponsor have to do?" Claire asked.

"The sponsor has to write a letter on Vivian's behalf," Annette said, "stating why he or she thinks the girl would be a good candidate for the program. The sponsor has to take a class with her once a week, has to make sure she understands what's required of her. The sponsor has to spend another three hours each week with Vivian and Haley both, helping them just live a normal life. Taking them to the grocery, the playground, whatever. I don't want to say it's baby-sitting duty, because it's really a lot more than that. But the sponsor does play an active role in their lives.

"For that reason, it needs to be someone who's willing to make a substantial contribution of time and emotion," she concluded. "And for that reason, a lot of people are hesitant to get involved."

"I'll be Vivian's sponsor," Nick said immediately, surprising himself as much as he'd clearly surprised Annette and Claire.

"You?" the social worker replied dubiously. "But—"

"I'd be perfect," he said. "I'm a cop—a public servant. I'm no stranger to volunteering with youth programs. I already have a relationship with Haley. I can fit the time into my schedule with no problem. I can do this," he stated adamantly. "I can help her. I can make a difference in both their lives."

He could, he realized. This was a real opportunity to do something worthwhile, something that would reap positive—and very clear—benefits. Nick *could* make a difference, in Haley's life and in Vivian's. This was exactly the kind of thing he'd always wanted to do, and precisely what he was failing to accomplish in his police work. He'd be crazy to turn down this opportunity.

"I want to do it," he told Annette with conviction. "I want to help them out. God knows no one else has ever given Vivian a break. She deserves this. She needs this."

And so do I.

The thought jolted him at first, then Nick decided he shouldn't be surprised by it at all. Vivian had been right on the mark when she'd assessed the way that Claire had set up her life based on her need to take care of others. And Nick was just now beginning to realize that he'd done exactly the same thing.

From the minute he'd entered the police academy, his ultimate goal had been to become a narcotics detective. He'd wanted the position because he'd wanted to work with kids—had wanted to help them stay clean and find ways to cope with reality that didn't poison their systems. Likewise, all the volunteer work he'd ever done with the police force had focused entirely on youth programs.

He'd surrounded himself with opportunities to work with

kids, because he'd wanted kids of his own and had known he would never have them. Maybe it had all been subconscious, but it all made sense to him now. Subconsciously he'd known he would always be in love with Claire. If he couldn't have her, he didn't want anyone else. And if he didn't want anyone else, then he'd never have a family. So he'd created a family for himself through his work.

It was all so obvious to him now. He felt almost foolish for not having realized it a long time ago. And now it was obvious that Claire had done the same thing. She'd created a family from the other remnants of her life, because she'd been too frightened to start one of her own.

Well, well, well. What *were* they going to do with each other?

Although Nick had one or two ideas in that respect, he pushed them aside for the time being. He switched his gaze from Annette's to Claire's and smiled. "Ask Claire," he told the social worker. "She'll tell you I'm good with kids."

Claire smiled back. "He's the best," she said. "I couldn't have managed Haley without him. Someday he'll be a wonderful father."

"Someday soon, I hope," he returned, his gaze never faltering from Claire's. He only prayed that he wasn't pushing his luck.

Claire said nothing to comment on his remark, but she continued to smile at him in a way that gave Nick much hope for the future.

They were going to do it, he thought. They were going to come out of this thing okay. Somehow, some way, the two of them were going to figure out a way to make everything work. They really did want the same things. They just hadn't realized it until now. It had taken the presence of a baby and a too-savvy teenager to make it all come clear, but clear it was. He wasn't sure yet what all it would take, or how far the two of them would have to bend, or how long it would be before they could see eye-to-eye on a lot of things.

But they were going to do it, he told himself again. They were. Somehow.

"Sign me up, Annette," Nick told the social worker confidently. "I'll be Vivian's sponsor, and I'll see to it personally that she and Haley get through the program with flying colors."

Annette chuckled at his enthusiasm. "You know, Detective, I think you will. There's some paperwork I'll need to put in motion, and I can do that right now, if you can hang around for a little while. Nothing personal, but we'll have to run a background check on you, and—" She laughed harder at the sputter of indignation he expelled, then added as she rose from her chair, "Don't worry. It's just a formality. I have nothing but confidence in you. Give me ten minutes to get all this rolling. I'll be back."

And with that she made her way toward and through the door, leaving Nick and Claire on their own.

It was going to work, he thought again, meeting her gaze levelly across the table. He would do whatever it took to ensure that. All that mattered now was Claire. As long as he had her, everything else would be okay. Everything.

"Marry me, Claire," he said suddenly, impulsively, grinning at the sheer, unadulterated panic that filled her eyes when he did.

"What?" she demanded.

"Marry me," he repeated, his grin broadening as he realized now how simple the whole thing was. "C'mon," he cajoled. "You know you want to."

She gaped at him, two bright spots of pink staining each cheek. "But—but—but…"

"Hey, you love me, right?" he said.

"I—I—I..." She seemed to realize it would be pointless to deny it, so she replied in a very soft voice, "Yes. I do love you. But Nick, there's so much more we have to—"

"And I love you," her interrupted her. "You know that, right?"

"I—I guess so."

"You *know* so," he corrected her confidently. "Don't gimme this 'I guess so' stuff. I know you too well."

She smiled tenderly at him, an encouraging sign. "Yes," she agreed in that same soft voice. "I know you love me."

"Then marry me."

She said nothing for a moment, only sat there staring at him as if she couldn't quite believe he was real. Nick's heart pounded hard behind his ribs, and a roar of heat rushed through him as he waited to hear her answer. He was dizzy and hot, and he didn't know what he would do if she told him no. She wouldn't tell him no, he assured himself. She couldn't. They'd been through too much over the last twelve years for her to deny them a future together now.

"But Nick," she said, skirting the question, something that did *not* escape his notice, "there are so many things we need to settle before we can make a commitment like that to each other. We haven't even spent two full days together. And we still have twelve years' worth of separation to contend with. We have way too much to talk about before we can bring up a topic like...like..." She swallowed hard, but she didn't look away. "Like...marriage."

He couldn't believe she was still worried about all that stuff. "The only thing we need to know, Claire, the *only* thing, is that we love each other. Period. Everything else will work out because of that. I promise you."

She hesitated before speaking, nibbling her lip with much

thought. "You seem so positive that that's all we need. You make it sound so simple."

"It *is* all we need. It *is* so simple."

"I don't know…" she hedged. "It seems so complicated to me. I don't know how we're going to compromise on all of it. There's a lot that hasn't changed between us."

"We'll compromise," he assured her. "Trust me."

"But how?" she insisted. "How can we compromise on the things we need to compromise on?"

"Just trust me, Claire, for once in your life." He reached across the table and curled his fingers over hers. "Marry me," he said again, more insistently.

She gazed down at their hands for a long, long time without speaking. Then, very slowly, very tentatively, she entwined her fingers with his. "I think you're crazy," she said softly, glancing up to meet his gaze. "But I guess I am, too. Okay," she finally relented, and the explosion of relief in his belly fireballed through his entire body. "I'll marry you. But you had better know what you're doing, Nick. 'Cause I certainly don't."

"No problem," he assured her, laughing out loud when was unable to quell his joy. "We'll work it out, Claire. I promise you we will. You and me, we'll have everything we've ever wanted. Everything. Trust me."

Epilogue

Claire stepped dripping wet out of the shower and glanced down at the gold wristwatch that glittered on the bathroom vanity. Great. She was going to be late for work. Again. She couldn't remember the last time she'd managed to get to the office exactly on time, never mind early.

Oh, wait. Yes, she could, too, remember. The last time she'd managed to make it to work early had been way back before Nick had entered her life again. Back then, she'd simply had no incentive to remain in bed once that alarm went off in the morning. These days, however, even the alarm couldn't make them get up. Not until they were finished—

Well. She smiled as a wicked warmth wound through her body. Too bad she was running late, otherwise she and Nick could just… Then again, the reason she was running late was because she and Nick had spent way too much time…

Oh, never mind, she told herself. No sense dwelling needlessly on something that wasn't going to happen. Not this morning, at any rate. Not again. Three times would, after all, be pushing it.

Quickly she toweled off and dried her hair, then began the usual morning search for her cosmetics in the linen closet. She pushed aside a rubber ducky—which squeaked its indignation at being handled so roughly—bypassed a Big Bird float toy, shoved aside a stack of washcloths depicting the Little Mermaid, Barbie, Spiderman and G.I. Joe, then finally located her cosmetic bag beneath a massive Lego construction that was slightly mottled with soap scum.

Honestly. She'd told Nicky time and time again not to take his Lego blocks into the bathtub, but did he listen? Oh, sure, he listened. He listened with all the enthusiasm of a five-year-old boy. And Nick was no help. Nick was the one who'd assured Nicky that Lego blocks were bathtub safe in the first place.

Hastily Claire completed her toilette, then moved out into the hallway, easily dodging a pair of pink plastic roller skates and a small pile of Beanie Babies as she went. "Delaney!" she called out to her seven-year-old. "These roller skates do *not* belong in the hallway. Molly!" she added for the benefit of her three-year-old, "I'm taking Snip and Dot and Bruno to the Beanie pound if you don't keep them in your room where they belong!"

Satisfied that she'd handled the problem, Claire continued on to the bedroom she shared with Nick, and quickly dressed for work in a plum-colored suit and ivory shell. She shoved her feet into low-heeled pumps, then exited as she fixed small pearl studs into her ears. She and her partners were interviewing a new OB-GYN today, seeing as how the practice had expanded so much in the last few years, and she wanted to afford the proper image.

She heard the normal ruckus from the kitchen before she even entered, so the sight that greeted her eyes by no means surprised her. Child-induced chaos was standard operating procedure on the Wainwright-Campisano homestead. And besides, as always, Nick had everything under control.

He was born to be a father, she thought. Full-time. Even with four little Campisanos to keep track of, he always had the place running like clockwork. This morning was no different. While Nicky scooped up a pile of spilled cereal, Molly sat at the table watching him, finishing off her chocolate milk. Delaney stood at the counter beside Nick, drying the dishes he'd just finished washing, and Nick had seven-month-old Joey propped against his shoulder, urging him to burp.

All but the baby were dressed and ready for school, kindergarten or preschool, and each of their backpacks hung like soldiers from their respective hooks by the back door. Without even looking, Claire knew those backpacks would be filled with lunches and homework assignments and whatever else it was that Nick made sure went in them every morning. He was amazingly adept at seeing to the children's needs. And hers, too, she added to herself with a smile.

"Your lunch is in the fridge," he said when he saw her, detecting her thoughts, as always.

He hadn't showered or changed yet, and stood barefoot, cradling the baby, wearing striped flannel pajama bottoms and a white, V-neck T-shirt. Wednesday wasn't his car pool day, so he could take his time getting dressed this morning. Of course, once the kids went off to school, he'd have his day filled with other obligations. Grocery. Laundry. Yard work. The usual. They tried to share the children's extra-curricular obligations—Kindermusik, soccer practice, ballet and piano lessons—but Nick always seemed to catch the brunt of that, too.

He just looked so incredibly scrumptious standing there, this husband of hers, all bed rumpled and unshaven, surrounded by the warm wonder of their children. A big, burly, handsome man with the tenderness and gentleness and nurturing nature of a father. It was just too, too sexy to resist. Claire wanted nothing more than to curl herself into him and just hug him for an hour or so. She hoped he knew how very much she loved him. Judging by his smile, she was pretty sure he did.

"You are, without question," she said, "the absolute…" She hesitated, sparing a glance toward the children. "*S-e-x-i-e-s-t,*" she spelled, "man in the entire world."

"Ew!" Delaney piped up. "You think Daddy's sexy? But Mommy, he's still in his pajamas! And he hasn't even shaved yet! Yuck!"

Yum, Claire mouthed silently in correction. To her daughter, she said, "No more cable TV for you, young lady."

Delaney gaped, her dark eyes flashing her outrage. "But Mom!"

Nick just smiled. "I hope you don't mind leftover roast beef on your sandwich," he said, steering them back into safer conversational waters.

"Are you kidding?" she asked as she approached the coffeemaker. She deftly dodged both a ball and an airborne strawberry as she went. "Stop it, Nicky. Food stays on the plate or in the mouth, Molly." Then, without missing a beat, to Nick, she added, "I love your roast beef. You know that."

He shrugged. "Yeah, but I made the same thing for your lunch yesterday."

She chuckled. "You're apologizing for making me

lunch,'' she pointed out. ''Do you realize how ridiculous that is? Do you know how many women would sell their souls to be in my position?''

He grinned lasciviously. ''Yeah, well, I can imagine a couple of positions I'd like to—''

''Not in front of the children, Nick.''

He laughed harder. ''Yeah, yeah, yeah. I'm fixing lemon chicken for dinner tonight, so you might want to pick up a bottle of white on your way home.''

''Done,'' she said, sipping her coffee carefully.

''And don't forget we have the school open house tomorrow night.''

She squeezed her eyes shut. ''I forgot all about it. Thanks for reminding me.''

''Yeah, it oughta be interesting,'' he added, wiggling his eyes playfully. ''Jeannie Distefano is gunning for me big-time.''

This was news to Claire. Naturally, Jeannie Distefano's Gestapo PTA tactics were legendary around Rushmont Elementary School, but she'd never picked on the Wainwright-Campisanos before. ''Why?'' she asked.

Nick rolled his eyes. ''’Cause Louise Phillips put me in charge of the bake sale this year. Jeannie doesn't think I can handle it because I'm a man. She's such a sexist. It's so stupid.''

Claire couldn't help laughing. Only Jeannie Distefano would take on the likes of Nick Campisano. ''You've been active with the PTA for a long time now, Nick. You knew the job was dangerous when you took it.''

''Yeah, well, some of those school moms are just a tad power hungry.''

''Mmm,'' Claire said noncommittally.

''Oh, and I suppose you think *I'm* one of 'em, huh?''

''I never said that.''

"Just because I demanded a recount last year for the PTA presidency."

"I never said a word."

"I only lost by fifteen votes, Claire. I just wanted to make sure everything was on the up-and-up, that's all. Jeannie's fully capable of ballot stuffing, and you know it."

"Mmm."

"Anyway, don't forget the open house. Vivian said she'd be glad to come over and watch the kids. And she's bringing Haley with her, which should make Delaney and Molly happy. Man, that kid has grown. I can't believe she'll be starting middle school next year."

"And Vivian will be finishing up law school at the same time," Claire added, still amazed that Vivian had come so far. Of course, Nick's sponsorship—and their friendship—had helped a lot. "*And* she's getting married. Which reminds me that I need to call her about the florist."

"Yeah," Nick agreed, "it's nice she met Stephen when she did. He's a good guy. And it's great to finally see everything working out for her. She's a good kid, and she's worked hard. She deserves to be happy."

"Like us," Claire said with a smile.

Nick smiled back. "Yeah. Like us."

She arrowed her brows down in concern. "You sure you don't have any regrets about quitting your job to be a dad full-time?"

He chuckled with genuine happiness. "Not for a minute," he assured her, as he always did when she asked such a question. "Claire, the job I have now is so much more important than the one I had before. You know that."

She nodded, reassured. "Yes, I do. I just want to make sure you know that, too."

He nuzzled the downy head of the baby in his arms, then

arced his gaze around the kitchen, over each of their boisterous children in turn. "Yeah, I do. Believe me, I do."

Their compromise had worked out beautifully, Claire thought. Mainly because they hadn't had to compromise at all. They'd both gotten exactly what they'd wanted all along. Claire had her career as a physician, and a beautiful family to call her own. Nick had his career as a father, and a beautiful family to call his own. He was providing the perfect role model, and making a difference in the lives of children—his own.

The house she had bought years ago, with what she now realized had been a subconscious hope that she would someday fill it with the laughter of children, was overflowing with that and so much more—with love and life and happiness and pure, unadulterated contentment.

Who said you couldn't have it all? she wondered. Because she and Nick had gotten everything, *everything,* they had both ever wanted. No way did life ever get any better than this.

And no way would she trade it for anything.

* * * * *

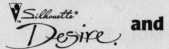 

Desire

These women are about to find out what happens
when they are forced to wed the men of their dreams
in **Silhouette Desire's** new series promotion:

The Bridal Bid

Look for
the bidding to begin
in **December 1999** with:

GOING...GOING...WED! (SD #1265)
by **Amy J. Fetzer**

And look for
THE COWBOY TAKES A BRIDE (SD#1271)
by **Cathleen Galitz** in **January 2000:**

Don't miss the next book in this series,
MARRIAGE FOR SALE (SD #1284)
by **Carol Devine,** coming in **April 2000.**

The Bridal Bid only from **Silhouette Desire.**

Available at your favorite retail outlet.

Silhouette®
Where love comes alive™

Return to romance, Texas-style, with

ANNETTE BROADRICK

DAUGHTERS OF TEXAS

When three beautiful sisters round up some of the Lone Star State's sexiest men, they discover the passion they've always dreamed of in these compelling stories of love and matrimony.

One of Silhouette's most popular authors, **Annette Broadrick** proves that no matter the odds, true love prevails.

Look for **Daughters of Texas** on sale in January 2000.

Available at your favorite retail outlet.

Visit us at www.romance.net

PSBR3200

SILHOUETTE'S 20TH ANNIVERSARY CONTEST
OFFICIAL RULES
NO PURCHASE NECESSARY TO ENTER

1. To enter, follow directions published in the offer to which you are responding. Contest begins 1/1/00 and ends on 8/24/00 (the "Promotion Period"). Method of entry may vary. Mailed entries must be postmarked by 8/24/00, and received by 8/31/00.

2. During the Promotion Period, the Contest may be presented via the Internet. Entry via the Internet may be restricted to residents of certain geographic areas that are disclosed on the Web site. To enter via the Internet, if you are a resident of a geographic area in which Internet entry is permissible, follow the directions displayed on-line, including typing your essay of 100 words or fewer telling us "Where In The World Your Love Will Come Alive." On-line entries must be received by 11:59 p.m. Eastern Standard time on 8/24/00. Limit one e-mail entry per person, household and e-mail address per day, per presentation. If you are a resident of a geographic area in which entry via the Internet is permissible, you may, in lieu of submitting an entry on-line, enter by mail, by hand-printing your name, address, telephone number and contest number/name on an 8"x 11" plain piece of paper and telling us in 100 words or fewer "Where In The World Your Love Will Come Alive," and mailing via first-class mail to: Silhouette 20th Anniversary Contest, (in the U.S.) P.O. Box 9069, Buffalo, NY 14269-9069; (in Canada) P.O. Box 637, Fort Erie, Ontario, Canada L2A 5X3. Limit one 8"x 11" mailed entry per person, household and e-mail address per day. On-line and/or 8"x 11" mailed entries received from persons residing in geographic areas in which Internet entry is not permissible will be disqualified. No liability is assumed for lost, late, incomplete, inaccurate, nondelivered or misdirected mail, or misdirected e-mail, for technical, hardware or software failures of any kind, lost or unavailable network connection, or failed, incomplete, garbled or delayed computer transmission or any human error which may occur in the receipt or processing of the entries in the contest.

3. Essays will be judged by a panel of members of the Silhouette editorial and marketing staff based on the following criteria:

> Sincerity (believability, credibility)—50%
> Originality (freshness, creativity)—30%
> Aptness (appropriateness to contest ideas)—20%

Purchase or acceptance of a product offer does not improve your chances of winning. In the event of a tie, duplicate prizes will be awarded.

4. All entries become the property of Harlequin Enterprises Ltd., and will not be returned. Winner will be determined no later than 10/31/00 and will be notified by mail. Grand Prize winner will be required to sign and return Affidavit of Eligibility within 15 days of receipt of notification. Noncompliance within the time period may result in disqualification and an alternative winner may be selected. All municipal, provincial, federal, state and local laws and regulations apply. Contest open only to residents of the U.S. and Canada who are 18 years of age or older, and is void wherever prohibited by law. Internet entry is restricted solely to residents of those geographical areas in which Internet entry is permissible. Employees of Torstar Corp., their affiliates, agents and members of their immediate families are not eligible. Taxes on the prizes are the sole responsibility of winners. Entry and acceptance of any prize offered constitutes permission to use winner's name, photograph or other likeness for the purposes of advertising, trade and promotion on behalf of Torstar Corp. without further compensation to the winner, unless prohibited by law. Torstar Corp and D.L. Blair, Inc., their parents, affiliates and subsidiaries, are not responsible for errors in printing or electronic presentation of contest or entries. In the event of printing or other errors which may result in unintended prize values or duplication of prizes, all affected contest materials or entries shall be null and void. If for any reason the Internet portion of the contest is not capable of running as planned, including infection by computer virus, bugs, tampering, unauthorized intervention, fraud, technical failures, or any other causes beyond the control of Torstar Corp. which corrupt or affect the administration, secrecy, fairness, integrity or proper conduct of the contest, Torstar Corp. reserves the right, at its sole discretion, to disqualify any individual who tampers with the entry process and to cancel, terminate, modify or suspend the contest or the Internet portion thereof. In the event of a dispute regarding an on-line entry, the entry will be deemed submitted by the authorized holder of the e-mail account submitted at the time of entry. Authorized account holder is defined as the natural person who is assigned to an e-mail address by an Internet access provider, on-line service provider or other organization that is responsible for arranging e-mail address for the domain associated with the submitted e-mail address.

5. Prizes: Grand Prize—a $10,000 vacation to anywhere in the world. Travelers (at least one must be 18 years of age or older) or parent or guardian if one traveler is a minor, must sign and return a Release of Liability prior to departure. Travel must be completed by December 31, 2001, and is subject to space and accommodations availability. Two hundred (200) Second Prizes—a two-book limited edition autographed collector set from one of the Silhouette Anniversary authors: Nora Roberts, Diana Palmer, Linda Howard or Annette Broadrick (value $10.00 each set). All prizes are valued in U.S. dollars.

6. For a list of winners (available after 10/31/00), send a self-addressed, stamped envelope to: Harlequin Silhouette 20th Anniversary Winners, P.O. Box 4200, Blair, NE 68009-4200.

Contest sponsored by Torstar Corp., P.O. Box 9042, Buffalo, NY 14269-9042.

ENTER FOR
A CHANCE TO WIN*

Silhouette's 20th Anniversary Contest

Tell Us Where in the World
You Would Like *Your* Love To Come Alive...
And We'll Send the Lucky Winner There!

Silhouette wants to take you wherever
your happy ending can come true.

Here's how to enter: Tell us, in 100 words or less,
where you want to go to make your love come alive!

In addition to the grand prize, there will be 200
runner-up prizes, collector's-edition book sets
autographed by one of the Silhouette anniversary
authors: **Nora Roberts, Diana Palmer,
Linda Howard** or **Annette Broadrick**.

DON'T MISS YOUR CHANCE TO WIN!
ENTER NOW! No Purchase Necessary

Silhouette®
Where love comes alive™

Name:

Address:

City: State/Province:

Zip/Postal Code:

Mail to Harlequin Books: **In the U.S.**: P.O. Box 9069, Buffalo, NY
14269-9069; **In Canada**: P.O. Box 637, Fort Erie, Ontario, L4A 5X3